Acknowledgements

The author wishes to acknowledge the support of the Arts Council of Ireland, of his parents, Kevin and Josephine, and of his many friends.

Special thanks to Jonathan Williams for his understanding, professionalism and guidance, and to all at Poolbeg who have worked on the production of this book, especially Nicole Jussek, Nicole Hodson, Brenda Dermody, Ann Marie Durkan and Elaine Kennedy.

Míle buíochas also to the marvellous Bernard and Mary Loughlin in Annaghmakerrig.

With love to my brother, Peter, and sister, Úna,
to Valerie, who urged me to carry out this translation
and to the people of the cul-de-sac.

ECSTASY

"*I'm sorry to interrupt, Miss Naughton, but would you mind sending Úna Fitzgerald to the office, please? Úna Fitzgerald to the office, please. Thank you.*"

And, with that, the intercom cackled its way to silence once again.

"Oooooh!" came the taunt from the other girls in the class, some doing so out of pure malice, others simply because they didn't have the strength of character not to do so. And Úna reddened to the gills.

"Down you go, Úna," said Miss Naughton, Úna's French teacher.

"Come in," said Mrs McDonogh, hearing Úna's faint knock on the office door. Úna suspected that this call to the office had something to do with the new books for which she had not yet paid. Either that or the fact that, as of yet, three weeks into the new term, she still hadn't got the navy gym slip which they were obliged to wear. She had already concocted some excuse in her mind in the event of that being the issue. She opened the door and entered.

"Ah, Úna," said Mrs McDonogh, with that authority

1

which seems peculiar to school principals. She was seated at her desk. Alongside her stood the Vice Principal, John O'Neill, with whom Úna had always had a good relationship. He had taught her mathematics in both first and second year and she had always found him fair and friendly. But, more recently he had been made Vice Principal and his number of teaching hours had dropped considerably.

"Úna," he said, by way of saying hello.

"Mr O'Neill," said Úna.

"Sit down, please, Úna," invited the Principal.

And, as Úna sat, Mrs McDonogh stood and moved away from her seat. She moved to the coat stand which stood in the corner of the office, and removed a navy-coloured overcoat from it. It was one of the school uniform coats. Then she approached the desk again and extended the overcoat towards Úna.

"I believe that this is your overcoat, Úna. You seem to have left it behind you by the basketball court yesterday afternoon. The caretaker noticed it when he was crossing the schoolyard."

Úna took it from her and looked at the lining inside the collar where she had written her name.

"Yes, Mrs McDonogh, it is. Thank you very much." She was very courteous in her speech, but also very nervous. At this point she had no idea what this summons to the Principal's office was all about and even less of an idea as to what her overcoat had to do with anything.

"Would you mind emptying the contents of the pockets out on to the table, Úna?" asked Mr O'Neill.

Úna's mind busily tried to recall what, if anything, she might have in her pockets. A paper hankie, she suspected, some money for the bus, she thought, and keys. That would be about it, she figured. She stood now and began to do as he had requested. Her memory had served her well: hankie, money, keys and, along with them, a slide for her hair and a library ticket. Once emptied she looked at the two teachers.

"And now the inside pocket, Úna, if you please," said Mrs McDonogh.

"Inside pocket . . . " repeated Úna.

"Yes, Úna, the pocket in the lining."

Úna was bemused at this. In the lining! She had never even realised that there was a pocket there. She rooted a little in the lining and, sure enough, there it was, a pocket as obvious as any other pocket in the coat. She looked at the teachers and smiled a smile that was a mixture of surprise and nervousness. But neither of the teachers showed even the slightest hint of a smile. In fact, if anything, their looks were looks of seriousness, cold and stoic. Úna slipped her hand into the pocket and felt one or two things inside. She took them out: two sweets, it seemed, wrapped in that greasy type of white paper that's often used for lozenges. They were like Rennies, really, except that they seemed to be somewhat more rounded.

"Now, if you would please," said the Principal, extending her open hand towards Úna and gesturing to her to put the contents of the pocket in her open palm. Úna did so.

"Now, Úna, where did you get these?"

"In my pocket, Mrs McDonogh," said Úna unthinkingly.

The Principal's face reddened in anger at the apparent cheekiness of this response, but Mr O'Neill made a timely intervention.

"Now, Úna, there's no call to be smart."

As soon as he said this Úna realised that what she had said did actually have the appearance of being smart or cheeky. But that was not at all her intention – quite the opposite, in fact. It was nothing more than an innocence on her part that had led her to say so.

"Oh, I'm sorry," she said quite anxiously, "I didn't mean it that way. I wasn't thinking, Mrs McDonogh."

"Well then," said the Principal, "where did you get them?" Her face was stern, as rigid as it had been when first she had asked the question.

"I don't know, Mrs McDonogh. I'd never seen them until now. I didn't even know that there was a pocket in the lining until you mentioned it."

The teachers really couldn't determine whether what they were witnessing was the height of innocence, or whether Úna was conducting one major bluff. And, if it was a bluff, she was certainly doing it in the most convincing fashion. Certainly there was no evidence of her having given even the slightest iota of trouble since coming to the school some three years ago; but the teachers were all too well aware that, given large classes and the pressures of work, trouble could often slip by unnoticed for a time. And this particular problem had been one of major concern to all of the city's principals in the last few years and, despite their best efforts to nip it in the bud, things seemed to be growing steadily worse.

"But they're only Rennies or something like that, Mrs McDonogh," said Úna.

The teachers looked across at each other and, in their silence, both decided that, yes, this demonstrated extreme innocence on the part of Úna Fitzgerald.

Mrs McDonogh looked at Úna. "Yes, or something like that . . . " she said, and then looked over at Mr O'Neill once again.

"Sorry, Úna, to have taken you away from your French lesson," Mr O'Neill said, picking up the conversation and dispelling a little more of the awkwardness that had surrounded the discussion. "Now, if you don't mind all the same, we'd like to hold on to your coat for a wee while yet." And he turned back towards the Principal.

"There are a few spare coats in the storeroom, Mrs McDonogh. I'm sure Úna could borrow one of them for the time being."

"Oh, certainly, no problem whatsoever. Pick one for yourself on the way back to class, Úna," the Principal said, and she led Úna towards the office door.

Outside, at the notice-board, three of the fifth year girls were huddled together, whispering. Hilda Bergin, one of the heavies of the school, was among them. All three stared at Úna as she left the office, then huddled together again to continue their whispering.

Inside, in the office, the two teachers were weighing up the conversation.

"I really don't think she has anything to do with it," said John O'Neill.

"Well, I have to say that I agree with you, John,

particularly in light of what we've just heard. And, given her naivety and innocence, I think we did the right thing in not bringing up the question of the note."

"Oh, definitely. It's a good job that we had removed it from the pocket altogether. It's quite obvious that drugs are the last thing on her mind."

Both teachers then drew close to peruse the note again. In bold block letters it read:

THIS FIX FOR FREE – £12 IN FUTURE

Back upstairs Úna's mind was in a state of flux. She couldn't focus her attention on the French lesson. It was a double session and Miss Naughton couldn't help but notice how much at sea Úna was throughout. Fortunately, Miss Naughton had enough cop-on and tact to realise that whatever had gone on below in the office was still on Úna's mind. It was best to leave her to her thoughts for now, she figured.

And that, pretty much, is how it was throughout the day. Even by the time Commerce came around, the last class of the afternoon, Úna wasn't up to much in the attention stakes. The sense of relief she felt was great when, at last, the bell rang at the end of the day. Freedom! Thank goodness for that. It was the longest day at school that Úna could ever remember.

She was crossing the schoolyard when she heard her name being called. She turned in the direction of the call, and there, down by the entrance to the toilets, stood Hilda Bergin.

"Me?" said Úna, quite obviously surprised. Even the dogs in the street knew that Hilda wasn't exactly what you might call "a saint", and Úna, no less than anybody else, was wary of her.

"Yeah, you," said Bergin. "Aren't you Úna Fitzgerald?"

"Yes," replied Úna, nervously. Her apprehension was very evident to Hilda.

"Come here a second," said Hilda.

Úna was scared. In fact, if anything, she was more scared *not* to do as Hilda said than otherwise. She inched her way down towards her, filled with apprehension, and suddenly, just as she finally reached her, four other fifth years popped out from behind the little porch into the jacks. Suddenly Bergin grabbed Úna by the hair and pulled her head down, while, at the same time, she came up hard with a knee straight into Úna's face. Úna hadn't a clue what had hit her; all she knew was that her nose was spouting blood and she had heard a crack when Hilda's knee had made contact with it. Before she knew it, she was bundled into the foyer of the jacks and was being dragged in the direction of one of the sinks. The fact that the sink was already filled with water hardly registered with Úna until her head was ducked down into it. She could feel hands digging into the back of her neck and head, forcing her to stay beneath the water. All she could really do was to prance frantically with her feet and hope that somehow this would help the situation. But if ever she had made a mistake, that was it. One of the gang lashed out with a kick and caught Úna straight across the back of the calves with it. The pain went right up through her; the only reason she was still standing was that they were holding her up. They yanked her back up out of the washbasin and dragged her across the foyer to where Hilda was. Bergin then grabbed her by the hair again.

"Now get this, you little bitch, you," she said, "one word out of you about that E and you won't know what day of the week it is – *comprende,* huh?"

But Úna was totally out of it. Not only did she not get the drift of what Bergin was bellowing at her but, even if she did, she would still have been far too weak to muster up an answer.

"Comprende?" said Hilda again, and this time she unleashed a vicious puck into Úna's stomach, causing her to double up in pain.

"And if there's as much as a squeak out of you about any of what went on here today you'll be getting another little taste of it before too long."

And with that Hilda finished off the job by driving another of her haymakers hard into Úna's stomach, leaving her writhing in pain on the floor.

It was later that evening that the school maintenance man found Úna. She was lucky, really. A broken nose, a few loose teeth and a badly-swollen right eye. Then there was the usual procedure: the Principal's office, a battery of questions and then, when the gardaí were brought into it, there was even more questioning again. The fear of a lawsuit against the school was foremost in Mrs McDonogh's mind. She knew the Fitzgeralds to be reasonable people and, when Úna's parents were drawn in to the proceedings, the Principal was very much relieved to find that the notion of taking legal action did not figure in their thinking. Úna stayed tight-lipped throughout, claiming all the time that she knew nothing, that she didn't have the foggiest notion as to who might have been responsible for the beating.

Mrs McDonogh told Úna's parents and the gardaí about the tablets incident. She was virtually certain that the beating was related to that. But what could she do if Úna herself wasn't prepared to be more forthcoming about it?

"Nothing, really," the Garda sergeant told her. "We're perfectly happy to visit the school and to talk about any of these matters. Bullying, theft, drugs – we've specially-standardized talks on all of these issues, if that's what you want," he told the Principal. "But, as I've said already, unless someone is prepared to bring charges, or unless we catch the perpetrators redhanded, there's very little we can do about it. Our hands are tied. As it is at the moment, it is purely an internal matter."

◄○►

Of course, having someone running scared is food and drink to any bully, and Hilda Bergin was no different in that regard. When she realised how scared Úna was to tell the gardaí even the slightest detail, she knew that she could lean on her all the more. In no time at all she had Úna roped into distributing the stuff. It didn't take too many smarts for Úna to figure out how the two E tablets had first been planted on her. She knew that what she was doing was wrong, but it was one of those ugly vicious circles one falls into: the more she planted, the stronger the hold Hilda had on her and the greater her fear of her. A real Catch 22. Úna doing what she was doing because she was afraid not to do it. It was fear of fear that kept her at it, really. One of those "damned if you do and damned if you don't" situations.

One day, shortly after the Christmas holidays, the Principal and the Vice Principal visited all the classes and gave a talk. Just the day before, another girl had been beaten in the school but this time the beating had been far more severe than was the case with Úna. This girl had been hospitalised and was likely to be there for some time. Even the tiniest piece of information would be most welcome and could be crucial in resolving the matter.

Úna could feel her face reddening as she listened to Mrs McDonogh speaking. She knew deep down that it was the handiwork of Hilda and her cronies once again. She knew it all right, but she didn't have the courage required to say so. Fear pitted hard against courage and courage was vanquished. She knew what was right, but doing what was right was as difficult a task as trying to catch the wind.

Úna was out of sorts for the rest of that day. She couldn't get the thought of the girl who had been beaten out of her mind. Rekindled thoughts of her own beating didn't help matters any, either. And, even when she went home from school, her mind was still tortured by such thoughts – prodding, gnawing, pestering. She didn't sleep a wink and another day at school loomed ominously ahead.

The following morning Hilda and her crew gathered outside the school gates, as they often did. They appeared to be dispersing as Úna approached the entrance, but then closed in fast again, trapping Úna in the middle of their circle.

"Listen here, you little bitch," said Hilda, while, at the same time sinking her closed fist deep in beneath

Úna's ribs, if there's as much as a word out of you about any of this, you're a goner – is that clear?"

"Yes," said Úna sheepishly.

"I don't think I heard you clearly enough," said Hilda. "Did any of you hear her clearly, girls?" she asked, looking around at the others.

"Naw, Hilda, didn't hear anything," they said in unison, then tittered to themselves.

Hilda grabbed Úna by the front of her coat collar and pulled her towards her.

"Did you hear that, Fitzer? The girls here don't appear to have heard you," and once again the fist went hard and low into Úna's ribcage. "Do you understand that now, do you?"

"Yes, yes," said Úna, half crying, half speaking, but trying, above all else, to make sure that anything she said was sufficiently audible to satisfy Hilda.

It was the timely ringing of the school bell that spared Úna any further suffering.

Later that morning, midway through the maths session, when angles and hypotenuses were amongst the furthest things from Úna's mind, she touched the area beneath her ribs gingerly. The pain. It was quite bad. It was possible that a couple of her ribs were broken, she thought. Her mind was tortured wondering what she would do. What she *should* do was quite apparent to her, but should and would were miles apart.

The *should* was, she told herself, to go to the Principal and spill the whole lot out from start to finish. Otherwise things would simply continue to go from bad to worse. If only she had the courage to do it. Then it dawned on her that maybe someone else would come up-front about it all. But, in her heart, she knew that there wasn't really anybody else. It was just another of her efforts to escape the situation and, already, there had been more than enough of that.

"Do it now," said the teacher at the top of the class. The reference was, of course, to the mathematics in hand, but somehow the words registered in Úna's mind as an illumination of sorts, an intervention by fate to steel her nerve and steer her in the right direction. Yes, she would do what she knew to be right. She would do it. Up she got and headed out the classroom door, down the passageway, then down the stairs and finally she found herself at the door of the Principal's office.

She stood at the door, her hand aloft, ready to knock, when a voice interrupted her:

"Ah, ah, Úna!"

Úna turned. It was Hilda and two of her sidekicks, standing at the cloakroom door straight across from the Principal's office. Úna and Hilda's eyes locked hard on one another, Hilda's cold, grey eyes seeking to control Úna's weaker stare. A little palpitation crept across the lower rim of Úna's right eye and Hilda Bergin smiled cunningly at the younger girl.

"Úna," said Hilda once again, and she hardened her stare all the more. Then the memory of Hilda's fist driving itself in hard beneath her ribs came to Úna's mind again. She steeled her stare at Hilda. This time it was Úna who tightened her mouth and now she noticed that Hilda's smile had grown less confident. Hilda, the toughie of the school, smile waning now. Úna held her stare, then turned away and knocked three times, loudly and deliberately, on the office door.

"Come in," beckoned the voice of Mrs McDonogh . . .

RESOLVE

It was hard to believe that it was almost two years to the day since he had backed a horse. Two years come the 25th of March, to be precise. That was the last time that Alan Kelly had any truck with the nags. Four hundred quid he forked out that day. God, he'd never forget it for as long as he'd live. Four hundred quid on an old cart-horse of an animal called *Up and At 'Em*. He'd have made a tidy little bundle at odds like that: three to one! By the time the race started he had come into five to two. Sure, Alan thought he was on a hot thing at three to one, delighted with himself at having got him at the ante-post price. He'd been following the horse since first he saw him run at Sedgefield about a year before. The animal had been making steady progress since then. Alan was sure that he was on to a dead cert that day at Kempton. The going was firm – a good dry sod, and *Up and At 'Em* had already notched up a win at the same course.

Anyway, as things panned out, it really didn't matter what odds he got on him. The famous *Up and At 'Em* came a cropper two fences out and that was that. Alan couldn't believe it when he saw him hit the deck. He squeezed the bookie's docket so tightly in his hand that the nail on his index finger almost drew blood from his palm. The blackest day of his whole life, without the shadow of a doubt. Four hundred quid blown on a waster of an animal that was only fit for the knacker's yard. God, and how was he going to tell Sandra that he hadn't any wages to hand up to her on Friday?

That day was certainly a major turning point in his life and, looking back at it, perhaps it had come just in the nick of time. He was lucky not to have lost his job in the bar with all the inning and outing to the bookie's he'd been doing for years; leaving the various young apprentices who'd be on their CERT courses to run the bar while he legged it down to Coral's or Stanley's. He was blessed that Mike Davis, the owner of the pub, was as understanding as he was. Only for him Alan would have had an awful lot more than the loss of a week's wages to be worrying about – he could have been out on his ear, without a penny compensation.

Davis put it to him in fairly stark terms: a one-month rehabilitation course in the Rutland Centre or hand in his notice on the spot. With three kids and a wife to keep, it certainly wasn't going to be any joy-ride on the dole. He really had no right to expect that Davis would be so good to him, paying him the full whack each week while he was in the Rutland. Since then, he had thanked God time and again that he hadn't felt as much as the tiniest temptation to go near the nags.

Yes, the Rutland Centre certainly did the trick for

him. Up to then he had no control whatsoever over his gambling habit; it was as though it had him in a vice-grip. It wasn't that he didn't want to give it up – he did, of course; it was simply that, time and again, he was somehow inexplicably drawn to the horses, despite his regular resolve to try to buck the habit. It was as though he was driven by some insatiable little seed within himself – a seed, as they told him in the Rutland Centre, that could not be destroyed, but which he could learn to control rather than have it control him. That seed had ruled his life for far too long, had gnawed at him, had him at sixes and sevens with himself. And nowhere more than at home was the result to be seen: no proper furniture, no car, no telephone – all the things that every neighbour around them enjoyed. No money for school tours, and, worst of all, perhaps, the many times when there wasn't even money for food.

But that was all behind them now, thank God. Nearly two years gone and he hadn't felt the slightest twinge of temptation to even look at a horse; and anyway, where would be the sense in it when he considered the quality of life they had enjoyed at home since he gave them up. And now this year, for the first time ever, the prospect of a family holiday in the offing. Two weeks of glorious sunshine in Mallorca for himself and Sandra and the kids over the Easter holidays. And Sandra – she had been such a support, singing his praises so highly for having managed to put the money together for the holiday. He'd make the final payment to the travel agent today. That, of course, would necessitate leaving the bar, but for a far different reason to what used to be the case.

He placed his hand on the pocket in the backside of his trousers and felt the wad of notes that he had drawn from the bank earlier that morning.

"Two pints there, please, Alan," shouted one of the two men who had been nattering together at the far end of the bar.

"Right you be, Larry," said Alan, deftly slipping one glass under the Smithwicks tap and another under the Harp.

One thing's for sure, thought Alan, those boys were certainly discussing the nags. They were big into the racing scene but then they also had the money for it. Alan arrived with the pints, and, sure enough, it was horses-horses-horses non stop.

"That's one note I won't be putting on a winner's back," said Larry, handing Alan a fiver for the drinks.

"And maybe that's the way to have it, Larry," said Alan as he took it from him.

"Any luck yourself in Cheltenham, Alan?" asked Larry.

Alan beamed broadly – a beam of contentment – as he took the change from the till, then turned and slapped it down on the counter in that accomplished way that barmen have.

"Indeed and I didn't, and I won't either," said Alan, welling with pride as he said it. "It's nearly two years since I bothered with that crack. Sure you might as well be burning money."

"Really! Well, fair play to you," the second man said. Though Alan wasn't altogether sure, he thought Tom was this man's name.

"Two years come the end of this month," Alan continued, and he rested his elbow on the inside edge of the counter. "And I'll tell you something: if I never do another thing in life, I'll be eternally grateful that I managed to shake off that habit, anyway."

"Well, good on you," said Larry, "but I'll tell you this much, if ever a day was right for making a packet it's today. There's a French runner in the Gold Cup this afternoon, *The Fellow,* and a man would want to be a fool not to have a fair ould flutter on him."

Alan threw back his head and laughed at Larry's enthusiasm for the art of losing money.

"Right enough, he's a damned hot thing all right," said Tom, lending weight to Larry's opinion, "and one thing's for sure: if he doesn't come up trumps, I'm well and truly bunched."

"Ah here, lads," said Alan, "I'll leave it to you, and, when you make it big, would you ever remember the poor old slobs like me," and he moved away towards the other end of the bar, busily gathering empties from the counter top as he went.

Morning slipped into afternoon and, in the course of time, the horsey men at the top of the bar went off and were replaced by various other twos and threes who came and went. By now, of course, Barry, Alan's fellow worker, was also behind the bar. The lunch rush was over and they were taking advantage of the lull to have a quick bite to eat themselves before mid-afternoon business picked up again.

"Half past two, Barry" said Alan. "Listen, I want to head down to the travel agent's to pay off the remainder of that holiday money, and I may as well do it now before things get busy again."

"Oh, sure, Alan, bash away. I'll hold the fort. If things get hectic all of a sudden, you'll hear me roaring at the far end of Abbey Street." And they both laughed at Barry's attempt at being funny.

Alan and Barry worked well together and got on very well with each other, despite an age difference of twenty years or so. Each took a genuine interest in the other's life – Alan often asking how Barry was getting on with whoever his girlfriend might be at any particular time. It was either that or how was the team with which he played doing in the Leinster Senior League. And Barry too: to listen to him, you'd nearly think it was his own holiday in Mallorca, not Alan's – he had taken such an interest in it. He, more than most, knew just how much Alan deserved the break and the difference it would make to him to be basking in the Balearic sunshine, oblivious to the hustle and bustle back home in Dublin city.

It was ten to three when Alan finally got away from the bar. He sensed a marvellous air of freedom as he strode down by the Adelphi and by Independent House and on towards the junction with O'Connell Street. There was always a great buzz about the city at that time of day – car horns blowing at one another, people scurrying for buses or trying to get across the road before being run over by some ambulance which might be racing its way to an emergency on the other side of town.

As Alan neared the travel agent's office he saw Mike Davis coming towards him.

"I'm just taking two minutes, Mike, to pay off the balance on the holiday," said Alan. It was his way of assuring his boss that he wasn't up to anything else.

"Oh, that's fine, Alan. Take your time. I'll tell you one thing, anyway," he said, looking at the grey March sky, "you won't have to worry about it drizzling down on top of you when you're over there." And off he went, telling Alan that he'd see him some time later in the day.

Every now and then, as Alan moved along, he put his hand on the back pocket of his trousers, checking that the wad of notes was still there. The thought that, somehow, he might lose it after all the scrimping and scraping he'd gone through sent a shudder through him. No cause for worry though, it was there, safe and sound.

Just as he reached his destination an old acquaintance from his betting days, Enda Coyle, came out of a bookie's office which shared a common porch with the travel agent.

"Alan, me ould flower, how's it goin'? God, I haven't seen you in ages," said Enda, as he shook Alan's hand.

"Well, you can say that again, Enda."

"How are the gee-gees treating you these days – better than they're treating me, I hope?"

"They're not treating me at all these times, Enda," said Alan, and he proceeded to tell how he had finally kicked the habit. "Is that so!" said Enda, "Well, you're a better man than I am 'cos I can't get off them at all."

Enda reflected for a couple of seconds, wondering whether or not he should get off the question of horses, but the gambler's need to share his bit of news decided that issue for him.

19

"There's a French horse – an absolute certainty, if ever there was one – going in the Gold Cup this afternoon, Alan, and anyone with any sort of a nose for a winner at all should put his shirt on it. A guaranteed return if ever I saw one."

"Is that so?" said Alan, more by way of casually passing off the topic than allowing it to register too firmly in his mind. Still, he couldn't but be aware that it was something of a coincidence that this was the very same horse that the two in the pub had been on about earlier in the day.

Little else was said and Enda headed off, but he had already planted a seed in Alan's mind. Alan stood in the porch midway between the two doors. Imagine that, he thought. *The Fellow!* The very same horse, and all three punters so sure of him. Who was the trainer? Alan wondered. Not Mick O'Toole or Pipe or Johnjo anyway. No, it certainly wasn't one of the usual bunch if the horse was coming from France. But there was sure to be big money on him given that he was coming all the way from the Continent – that, in itself, told its own story. There was bound to be one of the top-notch jockeys on him: Adrian Maguire or Charlie Swan, maybe. Or maybe even Dunwoody. It dawned on Alan now that he had heard a number of customers recently talking about a real humdinger of a count-down between Maguire and Dunwoody for the Jockeys' Championship this year. The fact that he wasn't fully up to date on such matters brought home to Alan how successfully he had managed to distance himself from the whole racing scene. He didn't even realise that, more recently again, Dunwoody had been suspended and was ruled out of any participation in the Cheltenham Festival.

But Alan Kelly was oblivious to the fact that the old bug was getting a hold on him again. Of course, he realised that a vestige still remained and always would remain – that was the very nature of addiction – but he knew at the same time that he had things fully under his control. The sound of John McCrirrick's voice on Channel 4 inside made Alan smile. He could imagine him with his funny Sherlock Holmes hat and his mutton chops and all his tic-tac antics. Like him or not, there was no doubting that McCrirrick was a character. And he knew his horses too. Sure what harm was there in having a peek in, just to get the low-down on the French horse, and maybe have a quick look at the runners and riders . . . He'd be in and out in a jiffy. Again he felt the burly wad of notes in the back pocket of his trousers, then stepped into the bookie's office. As soon as he entered, that smell which is peculiar to a betting shop filled his nostrils, inviting him to come further into the heart of things.

In years to come a regular question in pub quizzes and on other such occasions will be "What horse won the 1994 Cheltenham Gold Cup?" And one thing is for certain: there'll be no one quicker with the answer than Alan Kelly.

UMBILICAL

*"The gardaí in Mill Street, Galway, are appealing to the
mother of the newborn baby boy found abandoned on
the steps of the Augustinian Church here in the city
centre to please make contact with them. The infant,
thought to be two to three days old, is reported by the
authorities in the city's University Hospital to be in good
health. It is also thought that the mother may be in
urgent need of medical assistance and senior Garda
officers have urged the mother to come forward and
assure her of every support and understanding.*

*In the Dáil today, the Taoiseach announced that his
meeting with the British prime min . . . "*

It took a huge effort for Ursula to make her way to the
TV, and even more again to accomplish the simple task
of pushing the on-off switch and banishing Ann Doyle
and *Six-One* news from the room. The screen closed up
into darkness, reducing itself at first to a bright white
cross in the centre, which too was quickly swallowed up
by the blackness. She summoned all her might and made

her way back to the bed. Once there, she gathered the quilt back in around her sides and shoulders. Thank God he's safe and well, she thought. At least now he would be cared for. Cared for far better than ever she could do if she had decided to keep him.

She slid her hand down beneath the sheet and gently felt her tummy. She felt quite sore: sore inside and out. It was almost as though she had a raw wound that burned at her insides. The birth had been much harder on her than she had anticipated, but she would be back to herself again before too long – she was sure of that. A story she had read shortly after she had learned that she was pregnant came to mind now. It was about the women of the Iroquois, the North American Indians, and how, when their time came, they would seek out a quiet place, crouch on their haunches and deliver the baby themselves. Then, once the birth was over, they would carry right on with the normal chores of the day. The thought of that bewildered Ursula. She certainly had not found it so easy.

At least the secrecy was over now, or the worst of it anyway, she thought. There were times throughout the nine months when she was sure her parents would have copped on to the pregnancy. Particularly her mother, she would have thought. Still, the elasticated waistband in the school uniform had served her well. And as for the sweater – she was lucky that loose-fitting clothes were all the rage: it gave her a whole new appreciation of floppy jumpers. And no morning sickness, apart from once or twice – that was a blessing. But the absolute icing on the cake was when her parents announced their intention to visit her only sister, Andrea, in Australia for the summer.

"It's the one and only advantage going with teaching – that three-month summer holiday," her father said, "the one and only."

Of course, they had intended that Ursula would come with them, but that was easily handled. Her suggestion to them seemed sensible enough that she might stay in Ireland, work a summer job, then spend the best part of a year in Australia with Andrea and her husband Greg before coming home again to start university. In fact, they seemed quite taken with the notion, particularly her father. He was forever saying that if ever there was "a kid who could be trusted" it was Ursula. My God, if only he knew the half of it!

She was amazed that, despite all the mental anguish, she had still managed to get through the Leaving Cert. Not only that, but she actually felt that she had done quite well in it. Time would tell on that one at any rate. Not long now – the results would be out the coming Thursday – the day before her folks were due back from Australia.

Perhaps the hardest thing about the Leaving Cert. was that Aidan, the father of the baby, was sitting straight across from her for the duration of the exams. She could see him sweating, drooping over the papers, when the last thing on his mind was academics. They had discussed the whole question of the baby when Ursula found out that she was pregnant. He had no interest in it, he said; wanted no hand, act or part in it. Anyway, that didn't matter to Ursula. She had already decided that she would look after the child, Aidan or no Aidan. The relationship had come to an abrupt end as soon as she had told him.

Aidan was in England for the summer. He had been promised work in one of those pea-processing factories. The nights were probably spent throwing back the pints, thought Ursula. That and God knows what else. Anyway, she really didn't care what he got up to. She had managed things quite well on her own, no thanks to him.

Eight minutes past nine. The nine o'clock news would be nearly half over. Out of the bed, over to the TV, push the button, then back into the bed again. The effort wasn't so demanding this time for some reason or other. Still, one of those remote control gadgets wouldn't go amiss.

Bryan Dobson was the reader this time round. It was odd but there was something in his face that always reminded her of Aidan . . . some little mannerism or other that they had in common. *"Gardaí in Mill Street, Galway, have again appealed to the mother of the baby boy left on the steps of one of the city centre churches to please come forward. They have given an assurance of strictest confidentiality and of utmost understanding towards the mother. A report from our Western Correspondent, Jim Fahy."*

Ursula pulled herself up in the bed a little. She was afraid to listen, and yet, at the same time, afraid to miss what it was that he might have to say.

"Gardaí here in Mill Street are still baffled tonight as to the identity or the whereabouts of the mother of the

25

*two- to three-day-old baby found on the steps of the
Augustinian Church here in the centre of the city. The
baby, a boy, reported to be in perfect health, was
warmly dressed, wrapped in a plaid woollen blanket and
carefully placed in a sheltered enclave inside the
archway of the main entrance to the church. Of more
immediate concern to the authorities at this stage,
however, is the health of the mother. It is felt that she
may be young, unmarried perhaps, and in need of
medical attention. Gardaí are appealing to her to make
contact with them and they are at great pains to
guarantee total confidentiality. They also urge anyone
with any knowledge of the mother to contact them at
Mill Street Garda Station. That's Galway, 091-563161.
That number again for Mill Street Garda Station:
Galway 091-563161. Now, back to you, Bryan."*

Again there was the relief of hearing that the child was
well. Ursula had taken such care to ensure that he would
be warm enough, that she would leave him in a safe
place and that it would be a place where he would be
come upon quite easily. There was great satisfaction in
knowing that that was how things had actually turned
out.

She turned off the TV again and lay back once more,
thinking of what had been said on the news. In time, the
heat and comfort of the bed made her a little drowsy and
she began to nod off. But still, her mind was full of
thoughts of all that had happened. She imagined his
small white hands – more fleshy than she would have
expected. And his little mouth: that little twist in his

upper lip when she tickled him under the chin. She could see so much of her own father in him when he looked like that. Wouldn't he be the proud grandfather to see himself so clearly in his grandchild!

This latter thought roused her from her half-sleep once again. For several seconds she could not be sure what was truth and what was imagining, such was the impression the thoughts had made on her mind. The thought crossed her mind that, perhaps, she had the choice to keep the child now. Oh no, don't start thinking that way, she cautioned herself. She had done the right thing, she assured herself; she had, she had. It was a good job she had abandoned the baby so early on. Otherwise a bond would have been formed and it would be impossible to do so. Where would be the sense in keeping him? It would only lead to heartbreak all round, most particularly for the child. No job, not even a qualification that might offer her the prospect of a decent job at some later date. She just couldn't fend for all the child would need. It would have been nothing short of naivety to have kept the child; nothing short of selfishness on her part.

She turned on to her other side in the bed, almost as if that would somehow shuffle up her thoughts and take her mind off the question of the baby. If so, the effort was in vain and the baby was still foremost in her mind. Her baby. She a mother. The joys of rearing him. His first little pants on him; his first tooth; first word, first step, first day at school! She smiled to herself as she imagined all the possibilities. But then the hard facts of reality represented themselves and she began to cry. She cried for a long time. The simple fact of the matter was that she had abandoned the child and, no matter what she might think now, she had done what was best in the circumstances. She wrapped both her arms around the pillow and cried. Eventually, it was only the discomfort of the wetness of the pillow against her cheeks that brought her to her senses once again.

Nearly half past ten. Time for *Network News* and Eileen Dunne. If she turned it on it would be sure to get her going once again, pricking and prodding her mind in exactly the same way as the earlier programmes had done. She decided not to; she wasn't able for any more. But that didn't stop the thoughts from flooding through her mind. Adoption would be the most likely outcome for the baby, she supposed. A good couple would take him, she hoped. That, at least, would mean that he would have some comfort in life. Her own harmless little innocent whose only sin was to have been born at all. And the woman of the couple: the mother, as it were. A mother in another mother's place. In her place, really; Ursula's place. Bathing, dressing, squeezing, kissing the soft little lips that Ursula should be kissing!

She burst into tears, sobbing, pining for her loss. The implications of what it was that she had done were coming home to her; the joy that she had rejected; the understanding that there was nothing selfish in the thought that she had something worthwhile to offer the little one. But now the chance was gone; too late to even try to retrieve the situation. Too late.

A drowsiness again, then into sleep. A cocktail of dreams played with Ursula's mind: Faces in and out – Jim

Fahy, Eileen Dunne, Bryan Dobson. "Utmost undestanding", "every support" and "total confidentiality," ... "563161" echoing around her mind. The smiling faces of her mother and father looking in at the baby in the cradle. And Ursula herself squeezing the baby tightly to her, stroking his hair and calling him her "little bundle".

3.14 am on the clock-radio. Another wakening. The thoughts she had been dreaming still fresh in her mind, her sense of motherhood keener than ever before. Renewed self-confidence stemming from these thoughts, impressing on her that the option she has taken is not the only one, that there is still time for a change of mind; that, maybe, letting the child go like that was not the best decision after all.

She gets up. Apart from her toing and froing to the TV, this is her first time out of bed since leaving the baby in the darkness of the archway in the early hours. She throws on a dressing-gown and looks again at the clock-radio: 3.27 am now. The exact time, unless she is mistaken, that she left her little baby son in the doorway of the church. One whole day. A mother parted from her baby son.

Downstairs in the kitchen, she can feel the coffee getting her blood racing once again. She moves into the sitting-room. The various family photographs in frames are lined up like soldiers on the mantelpiece. Herself and Andrea mainly – very few of her Mam and Dad. She lifts one of Andrea as a young baby. Hardly even a year old, she thinks as she looks at it. A little smile on Andrea's face – just to please the photographer, maybe!

A little twist in the upper lip, just like her father. Just like the twist in her own baby's lip, she thinks. She replaces the photograph on the mantelpiece and knocks back her coffee. She had better go to bed and get some decent sleep. She knows she will need all her energy when she goes down to Mill Street Garda Station later in the morning.

VANQUISHED

A week of worry and anxiety had left Owen Grogan exhausted. The room in which he sat was dour and grey – the perfect complement to the young teacher's state of mind. He felt very much alone, despite the presence of a garda in the room. It seemed strange to him that they felt it necessary to have a garda with him, as if he might harm himself in some way; or, worse again, harm somebody else. One of the court's clerical assistants had approached him earlier with a cup of coffee. And then a second cup for the garda, who seemed to welcome it every bit as much as Owen did his. It was nice of her, really, the clerk. She did it off her own bat, Owen thought.

"They won't be very much longer, I think," she said to Owen, then smiled at him. He looked at her as she left. It was hard not to be aware of her attractiveness.

What could be taking them so long in coming to a decision? Owen wondered. He knew the judge was inside with the lawyers. Talk, he supposed – what else? Lawyers and talk – two inseparable entities. He could use that one as one of those pairs he used throw out to the kids in Irish class: *The two most inseparable things in this world: a lawyer and talk.* Yes, that would be a good one to run by the students in 3B all right. But only good till one of the little smart alicks came up with two other things which were even more inseparable. And then you'd be pestered with that sniggering that some of them go on with. Just the type of thing that would play straight into the hands of the likes of Robson Byrne. Anyway, no point in thinking too much about that one. It was quite possible when the court handed down its decision that Owen's days as a teacher would be numbered.

Huh, Robson Byrne! The very reason Owen had found himself in court this past few days. What in the name of God had come over him to lose the head with the little brat? Not, indeed, that he didn't have good reason for doing so – Byrne had been nothing if not disruptive from day one – Owen at his wits' end trying to make his history lessons challenging and interesting while Byrne was doing his level best to create every form of mayhem. Then the others would feed off Byrne and add to the melee. But Christ, what possessed him to have lost the rag with him like that? Byrne's insult that day was just the straw that broke the camel's back.

"Would you ever get stuffed," retorted Byrne, when all Owen had done was to ask him to behave himself. And Owen lost the head. He could see it still: everything in a kind of slow motion playing itself over and over in his mind. *A History of the Soviet Union* by McClelland flying through the air; that ever-present sneer on Byrne's face and then Owen's stinging right hand making contact with the youngster's cheek. His only indiscretion in his ten years teaching. And the memory of it had haunted Owen ever since. As soon as he had done it he knew what the implications would be. Robson made straight for the door, then turned. "That's the biggest mistake you ever made, Grogan," he said, and he gave him the finger and sneered tauntingly at the teacher. Then he hightailed it straight to the principal's office and spilled out his account of things.

Owen was suspended from his teaching responsibilities on the spot until the matter came to court. The hands of the principal, David O'Doherty, were tied. He had no option but to follow the Department's directive on the matter and suspend Owen. It wasn't something that rested easily with O'Doherty, though it was some comfort to him that Owen realised there was nothing he could do other than follow the legal advice to the Department. It was nearly a year and three months now since Owen had stood before a class.

These past four days Byrne had sat there in the courtroom with that same obnoxious sneer etched permanently on his face. He was a much bigger young lad now than at the time of the incident. His parents either side of him and, funnily enough, that self-same sneer visible in the father's face. A chip off the old block, thought Owen. Not the slightest sign of nervousness about them as they sat there. Quite the opposite, in fact. If anything, they appeared confident, whispering amongst themselves and looking over at

Owen from time to time. Those were the times when the sneer was most obvious on the young lad's face.

The image of Byrne's face brought other details of the week to Owen's mind. His own testimony, for instance: he was kicking himself now that he hadn't fully taken the opportunity to tell the court of Byrne's endless troublemaking, every single teacher at some time or other at the morning coffee breaks going on about how their hearts were scalded with him, how there wasn't a day that he wasn't caught at some caper or other behind the school sheds. But the lawyer representing Byrne didn't really give Owen a proper chance to answer any questions fully: pushing, badgering, forcing him to give the answers that she wanted, but not the answers that Owen knew to be the truth.

"Tell me, Mr Grogan, are you a married man?"

"No."

"I beg your pardon. I'm afraid the Court did not hear you. Marriage, Mr Grogan – are you a married man?"

"No." Owen's speech was much louder the second time.

"No. No, Mr Grogan, you are not a married man. And would I be correct then in assuming that you do not have any children of your own?"

"That is correct."

"I see. It is correct to say that you do not have children of your own."

"Yes."

"And, Mr Grogan, would you have any real notion –

*as would a parent, say – of how best to deal with a child
who is contending with the difficulties of the trying
teenage years? Hmm . . . would you?"*

"Well, I suppose . . . "

*"It doesn't matter what you suppose, Mr Grogan.
Answer the question, please: yes or no."*

"Well, I think . . . "

"Yes or no, Mr Grogan. You would or you wouldn't."

"Well . . . "

*"A notion, as would a parent, Mr Grogan. Well, what
about that?"*

"Well, I don't know wh . . . "

*"So, you don't know, Mr Grogan. YOU-DON'T-
KNOW! You have a young innocent teenager in your
care for four, five, maybe even six sessions a week and
you admit to this court that you do not really know how
best to deal with him; that you really haven't got a
notion how best to handle him!"*

"I didn't say . . . "

*"That is all, Mr Grogan, thank you. I have no more
questions for you . . . except this one: did you strike –
did you assault this young and innocent teenager
without due cause?"*

"You don't understand . . . "

*"What I do or do not understand, Mr Grogan, is quite
immaterial here. Now, if you would simply answer the
question, please. Did you or did you not strike him?"*

"Yes, I did, but . . . "

*"So, you did, then. You struck this young teenager.
That's all for now, thank you. No more questions at this
point."*

That was day one – Tuesday. Things got even worse after that. The solicitor Owen had engaged couldn't hold a candle to the woman representing Byrne. God help us! Sure, didn't his own solicitor actually say to Owen that first day that he went to see him that the Court would more than likely side with a child in such a case, regardless of who was right or wrong. Talk about giving up the ghost before proceedings had even begun.

Wednesday. Fair play to David O'Doherty. He, more than anybody else, was attuned to Owen's predicament. It had always amazed him that some one or other of the teachers hadn't lost the rag with Robson Byrne and given him a bloody good hiding. When he thought of it, there was hardly a day that one of the teachers, at least, hadn't had occasion to send Byrne to the office for some reason or other. General disruption in the classroom was the norm with him, be that in the form of trying to upset the teacher or of distracting his fellow students. The absolute irony in the whole thing was that it was Owen Grogan who was the one to eventually hit him: the kindest, gentlest and probably the most conscientious member of the staff.

"To be quite honest with you, in all of my twenty-seven years as a school principal, I have not encountered a more capable, more conscientious and more dedicated teacher," O'Doherty said of Owen when questioned by the plaintiff's solicitor. He had just given similar testimony to Owen's own solicitor.

"Yes, yes, Mr O'Doherty, we heard this from you when you answered questions for the defence earlier on, but that has little or nothing to do with what it is that we

are discussing here," the lawyer said, *"and it most certainly does not answer the question which I have asked you, namely this: on the day in question, when my client Robson Byrne was assaulted – pardon me – allegedly assaulted by the defendant, was the history teacher, Owen Grogan, capable of keeping order in the class?"*

"Well, as I have already said . . . "

"We have heard what you have already said, Mr O'Doherty, but it simply does not address the question. Now, please, a simple answer: in your opinion, was Mr Grogan capable of controlling the class on the day in question? A simple yes or no."

"I do not know," said O'Doherty.

"Yes or no, Mr O'Doherty?"

"I do not know, I don't know."

"Exactly, Mr O'Doherty! You do not know. And would you like to tell the court, Mr O'Doherty, why you do not know?"

"Well, how could I possibly know? I wasn't there. I wasn't in the room when the incident occurred."

"Aha! My point precisely. Now we have come to the kernel of this evidence. You, Mr O'Doherty, were not there. You were not in the classroom. And therefore, it is impossible for you to say with any certainty – any certainty whatsoever – what actually happened on that occasion. Isn't that so, Mr O'Doherty?"

O'Doherty hesitated before answering. *"Well . . . "*

"Isn't it so, sir, hmm?"

"Well, yes, I suppose when you put it that way . . . "

"And so, is it not logical to deduce then that any

evidence you might give pertaining to the events within the classroom on that day can only be conjecture and must, therefore, be flawed? Is that not so, Mr O'Doherty?"

"Well, yes, I suppose. But I was called as a character witness, not as . . . "

"Thank you, Mr O'Doherty, for your co-operation. No more questions."

But why, wondered Owen, didn't the judge intervene at that point? Why did he allow the prosecution to trick David like that? If it was trial by jury the prosecutor's eloquence would surely have swung the day in favour of Byrne. Fortunately, as it was, the decision would be up to the judge. However, that statement by Owen's attorney the first day that they met, that the court is more than likely to favour the minor in such cases, still niggled at the back of Owen's mind.

Thursday: black and bleary Thursday. Despite Mr O'Doherty's best efforts on Owen's behalf the previous day, the prosecution had reduced his evidence to nothing. Even the testimony of others who spoke favourably of Owen – past pupils, fellow teachers, some parents, even – was twisted and thwarted by Robson Byrne's counsel; one could be forgiven for thinking that Owen Grogan was an out-and-out tyrant.

And Robson Byrne himself! That was the star performance of the day. So spruce, so well-dressed, well-mannered – exuding traits he had never shown before, certainly not in school at any rate. It nauseated

Owen to have to listen to him. He felt every "yes, sir" and "no, sir" from the little sleeveen like a stake being driven through his heart, made all the worse by seeing how obviously moved the judge had been by everything the boy had to say.

But worst of all on Thursday was the publicity, the dishonesty of the media. Owen was fearful of the negative effect their sensationalist reporting might have on his parents' health – they being quite old at this stage. Reporters, journalists, radio and TV people too. Just one long string of irresponsible reporting from day one of the hearing: *"Ground-breaking Hearing Today"* / *"I Struck The Boy – Teacher"* / *"Principal Admits Evidence is Suspect"*. And daily they followed Owen from the courthouse, firing questions left, right and centre at him. Thank God he had resolved before the hearing that, if nothing else, he would keep his cool and not allow the gnawing anger that he felt inside to show itself in public.

The opening of the door into the room, followed by a cool fresh breeze, shook Owen from his reverie. It was the clerical assistant back again. Owen looked down at his cup of coffee as soon as he saw her. The coffee now was as cold as the room itself. Owen, apart from having taken a sup or two from it, had totally forgotten about it. She herself looked down at the cup as she approached. Then she turned her gaze to Owen and smiled kindly at him.

"They are ready for you now, Mr Grogan. The best of luck," she said, and she squeezed his upper right arm as if to give him encouragement.

"Thank you," said Owen, forcing a smile. Then she was gone and there in her place was the guard who had been sitting silently in the room all the while. He now took hold of Owen's upper right arm. His grip was much firmer than the clerical assistant's, but was kindly nonetheless.

"Good luck," he whispered – the only two words he had heard from him all week long. He had a northern accent – Donegal, thought Owen. He steered Owen towards the door and on from there into the centre of the court.

Owen's lawyer was standing at the defence table, waiting to welcome him back. He looked ashen-faced, thought Owen. On the other side of the room were the Byrnes along with their repersentatives; they looked confident, particularly Robson. He turned towards Owen now and sneered in his usual manner.

The sound of a door closing at the top end of the room heralded the return of the judge and of his assistant who followed. The judge mounted the steps to his bench, sat, and began leafing through various papers, coughing a little every now and then. He pushed back his small rounded glasses on to the bridge of his nose, cleared his throat and spoke:

"I have given careful consideration to the facts of this case. Violence! Violence at the best of times is ugly . . . cowardly, indeed, be it the violence of one child towards another, of a man towards a woman, or even, indeed, of one man towards a second man."

You could hear a pin drop in the courtroom – everyone trying to guess from the judge's preamble what his decision might be before he'd actually announced it. Owen was despairing of the outcome already. He looked towards the members of the Byrne family and and saw how confident they seemed, as they were huddling in together and whispering to one another.

"But, ladies and gentlemen, the violence of an adult towards a child, and most particularly that of a man, is something that cannot in any circumstances be excused."

"Yes!" said Robson Byrne from the prosecution desk in the centre of the courtroom. It was that arrogant gesture of triumphalism that is so common amongst youngsters of his kind. The judge stopped, lowered his glasses from the bridge of his nose again and looked sternly in the teenager's direction. For the first time in the course of the days' proceedings he could see that snide sneer on the youngster's face. He recognised it as a sneer which told much about Byrne's make-up: a sly make-up. He raised his little hammer and came down hard with it on the small brass plate to the front of his desk.

"That's quite enough now, sonny," he said and he stared hard at Byrne, remaining silent for several seconds before continuing.

"The law is most clear in matters of this sort," and his eyes scanned the gathering as he spoke. "When children are left in the care of a school, in the care of a teacher, as is the case here, then that teacher is *in loco parentis*. They are left trustingly, in the confidence that that teacher will do nothing contrary to the trust which has been placed in him or her. It is quite obvious in this case, however, that that trust has been broken; that the plaintiff, Robson Byrne, has been subjected to violence and that, in being so subjected, an infringement has been made upon his rights."

Owen could see the last ray of hope to which he had been clinging peter into darkness. It was ironic that at his point of greatest weakness he should be dealt the cruellest blow.

"Will the defendant please stand," said the Judge. Owen stood, as did his counsel. His legs were like rubber beneath him.

"You, Owen Grogan, have been accused of violence towards Robson Byrne and it is the considered opinion of this court that you are guilty as charged."

Cheers and sighs from the body of the court showed the mixed reaction of those in attendance. Owen Grogan, however, was oblivious to any reaction other than that which he felt himself. It was as though the announcement went through him like an arrow, each word a jagged barb on the arrow-head. Those in the assembly quietened once again.

"I am imposing a fine of £500 on the defendant, Owen Grogan, as compensation to the plaintiff, Robson Byrne. The defendant is free to go but it is further the recommendation of this court that the Department of Education be advised to look again at the suitability of Mr Grogan for the profession of teaching."

This time exuberant shouts of joy came from the Byrnes and their supporters in the public gallery. Owen sat rigidly in his seat, again oblivious to the hubbub. The only hubbub to which his mind attended was that which he felt within: the hubbub of incredulity, of emptiness, of solitude. He didn't even see both attorneys come together alongside him, their handshake and their laughter at the sharing of some private little joke. It was only Robson Byrne standing directly in front of him that brought Owen Grogan back to his senses. There he stood, just as he had done that day one year and three months ago, and once again he made the same lewd gesture to Owen.

Night-time. Friday. Dark. The water in the canal looks deep and murky. Here and there light from the streetlamps catches the stillness of the water, but the figure on the bank is far removed from that. And cold. As cold as a cup of coffee from which very little has been drunk; as cold as a wooden hammer coming down hard on a little brass plate; as cold as a slab of marble or as death itself.

The darkness of the water spreads itself in gentle widening circles and makes the light reflected from the streetlamp dance fleetingly from one ripple to another.

Awkward

Nearly seventeen. My God, who would ever believe it? Seventeen years of age and he still hadn't had his first kiss. Talk about embarrassment! He was sick to the teeth this long time, listening to his friends, both at home and at school, boasting good-o about their exploits. There wasn't one of them hadn't had a girlfriend since second year. Every single one of them except for him. And a kiss! Huh! A kiss was nothing to them, if you could believe even the tiniest fraction of their boasting. Forever on about this one or that one who was good, or wasn't good, or who was better than a certain girl, but not nearly as good as some certain other.

Quiet. That was Dara's usual form when the lads would be comparing notes on girlfriends. There was, of course, the odd time when he would pitch in something or other to the conversation, just to give the impression that he wasn't in any way behind the door in such matters. But, in some respects, those times were even worse than spells of total silence because, somehow, he'd feel the extra pressure then of having drawn attention to himself. He would be better off not saying anything at all . . . but there was some little thing there, some inner pressure that seemed to egg him on to say something. A shut mouth catches no flies – maybe he'd be better to follow that rule. But then you had the other one about keeping an eye on the silent ones. God, he thought, how are you meant to win at all?

Ailbhe offers the open bag of wine gums to him.

"Would you like one?" She smiles. My goodness, she's beautiful-looking. Indeed, Dara is all too well aware of just how beautiful-looking she really is. More than any of the other girls in the school, Ailbhe is the one who the lads are forever on about. Imagine if they knew that he had actually asked her to the pictures.

"Would you like one?" she asks again.

"No, eh no – thanks." He knows his answer sounded awkward. The film is *Four Weddings and a Funeral*. He feels he wouldn't mind there being a second funeral if it would get him out of the dilemma in which he finds himself. *Four Weddings and Two Funerals*, he thinks. Hmm!

"Twelve screens, you know . . . "

"What? Sorry, what did you say?"

"Twelve screens," repeats Ailbhe. "They have twelve screens here in Tallaght."

"Oh – have they?"

Well, of all the bloody responses – "Oh – have they?" Hasn't she just blooming well told him they have. Why can't he think of something more inspiring than that to say to her? And now he's into chastising himself. What is wrong with him anyway that he cannot think of something normal, something sensible to say instead of that stupid "Oh – have they?" of his? Hadn't he already got over the hardest part by asking her out. Anything after that should be a piece of cake, he thinks. But then, maybe the psychological effort it took to muster up the courage to ask her out has taken its toll on him. It's either that or shyness. Well, of course – what else? Anyway, whether shyness or being drained of effort, he certainly feels himself at a loss in terms of making much of an impression on her.

"There are only ten in UCI at Coolock."

"I beg your pardon . . . ten . . . ten what?"

"Screens, Dara. Ten screens. Are you listening to anything I'm saying to you at all?"

"Yes. Yes, I am." And the poor divil was, God help him. But listening and hearing can be poles apart at times and, if truth were told, Dara has heard absolutely nothing of what Ailbhe has been saying to him. It is as if there's some little breakdown somewhere between his ears and his brain. Sitting so closely beside her has beguiled him, maybe. Instead of listening to what it is she's saying, his eyes are focused firmly on her lips as they move up and down with the words. Her lips – so soft, so red, so tempting. He wishes he could kiss them. Just kiss them – that's all. And indeed, he would, if only he could pluck up the courage.

"It's on in Coolock as well," she says.

He looks at her – mainly at her mouth. It's quite obvious again that he hasn't even heard what she has said.

"*Four Weddings and a Funeral* – on here in the Square and on in Coolock at the same time."

He smiles. God, he'd love to kiss her; just to taste her lips. He can just imagine how that one would go down at school, if they knew about it. His classmate, Brian Heffernan, or Casanova, as they call him, coming up to him on Monday:

"Well, Dara, any craic at the weekend?"

"Oh, nothing much, really. Naw, just kept it simple, Brian – you know yourself. Ailbhe and I went to see Four Weddings and a Funeral *on Friday. Out again then Saturday night and went for a pizza last night. Apart from that, a pretty quiet time. Mind you, I'm absolutely knackered for some reason."* And, as he says that, he can imagine himself stretching out his arms to really impress his tiredness on Heffernan.

"Ailbhe! Ailbhe O'Riordan?"

"Well, who else, Brian? Is there another Ailbhe?"

"You and Ailbhe O'Riordan!"

And Dara beams broadly as he imagines the look of amazement on Brian Heffernan's face.

"What are you smiling at, Dara?" asks Ailbhe.

Her question intrudes on his imagining and, suddenly, the magic of it all is dissipated. He blushes at the notion that, perhaps, somehow or other, Ailbhe is privy to the thoughts that have been running through his mind. Thank God for the semi-darkness of the cinema. Only for it, he'd be like a bright red beacon there beside her – even redder than Ailbhe's lips. Ailbhe's lips! Her lovely luscious lips! Oh, God!

"What are you smiling about?" Ailbhe asks again.

"Oh, nothing, nothing. Just a curious little thought that crossed my mind, then disappeared again," and now he assumes his look of shyness once again.

"Hmm!" she says, then slips her hand across the arm-rest, takes Dara's hand and squeezes it. Oh, my God! He doesn't know whether to squeeze it back or not. But then he does squeeze back, before he lets too much thought talk him out of it. And then he reddens once again. He senses Ailbhe's eyes fixed on him, but he resists the temptation to turn towards her. The fingers of their hands are still entwined. He doesn't know if that is as is best or not. Out of the corner of his eye he can see Ailbhe turn to face the screen again. That, in itself, is a relief of sorts. He turns slowly and looks at her: at her face, her mouth, her lips – lovely luscious lips.

The images on the screen are projected on to Ailbhe's smooth skin, the reflections dancing merrily all around her, weaving their way into the secret little crevices of her face. Shades of darkness, then of brightness intermittently filling the laugh lines on either side of her mouth. A shadow crosses her cheek and now another little one is playing with her bottom lip; flirting with Ailbhe's bottom lip, thinks Dara. His eyes latch onto the shadow at her mouth. A little tease of a shadow, really, moving up and down from lip to lip, and sometimes staying daringly between both lips. Dara's feeling as he looks at it is something of a mixture of jealousy and anger. Ailbhe raises her free hand and rubs her lips a little, where, obviously, some minor itch or tickle has irritated her. Her movement jolts Dara a little and prompts him to turn back towards the screen.

Oh no! There is a couple kissing on the screen now – yer man tasting the woman's lips, the wetness of her lips, the redness. He looks as if he knows what he's about – experienced, thinks Dara. Experienced, just like

Brian Heffernan and the rest of them at school, he thinks. Now Dara can feel the sweat on his palm in Ailbhe's hand. Should he pull away, he wonders. And, if he does, will he have the courage to take her hand again? Could she possibly be thinking the same things he is thinking? Oh, God, what possessed him to have asked her out in the first place? She probably only came because she pitied him. God, what he wouldn't give to have the ground open up and swallow him. If only he had the confidence, the daring, the courage to just give her one little peck on the lips. But he hasn't. He knows he hasn't and that he never will have, maybe. He nearly wishes he had never got himself into this.

But Ailbhe has kept a firm hold on his hand. Their hands are so tightly squeezed together now that he's not quite sure whether the sweat is on his hand or on Ailbhe's. This uncertainty is terrible for him. The dilemma for the male is never really appreciated in these matters, he thinks. He remembers reading something about that somewhere. Yes, the writer, whoever it may have been, said something about the onus always lying on the man. And it's always assumed that the man is fully confident; every man, even poor old Dara. God knows he'd give anything to get through this one. Or, if he wasn't meant to get through it, then let the big black hole open up right now and swallow him. That way, at least, the whole discomfort would be over and done with.

"Would you like another wine gum?"

Dara turns towards Ailbhe. Strange as it may seem, he has almost forgotten that she is there beside him. It is

49

the dilemma itself, much more than Ailbhe, that has confused him, and that, he thinks, is why he has forgotten that she is there. My God, she is so pretty. An absolute stunner, he muses as he looks at her. She gestures towards the bag of sweets where she has left them on the arm-rest.

"Would you like another one?"

Dara looks at the bag. He cannot even remember if he took one the last time she had offered.

"Yes, thanks," he says, and then, as soon as he has said that, he remembers having declined the offer the last time round. He reaches his free hand towards the bag and, as he touches it, a mixture of nervousness and awkwardness causes him to knock it off the arm-rest and down into the darkness of the floor between the two rows of seats.

The suddenness of it all causes Dara to involuntarily break his hold on Ailbhe's hand. Oh, no, it never bloody well rains but it pours is right. He feels like crying; feels like going down there after the sweets and never coming up again, safe in the seclusion of the darkness. He looks at Ailbhe; she looks at him. She is holding her hand up to her mouth, trying her damnedest not to laugh. Dara can feel his face go from red to purple with embarrassment. He feels like cursing, but, if he does that, he'll do it in the quiet of his mind.

By now, Ailbhe is in stitches, totally unable to hold back her laughter. Dara can sense the extreme heat of his own face as he feels the blood pumping hard against his temples. He turns away from her again and looks down towards the floor. His eyes adjust a little now to the

darkness down below. He can see the yellow of the bag
define its outline down there on the floor. He leans
forward a little, then lowers his head down into the
semi-darkness. In some respects, it is an effort to give
the impression of searching for the bag, but, in truth, it
is even more an effort to avoid the embarrassment of
Ailbhe looking at him as he reddens. Now Ailbhe too
leans forward, then down into the darkness, and, as she
does, she slips her right arm back across the arm rest
and takes Dara's hand again. Dara can feel his pulse
quicken once more. Now both faces are closer than ever,
down there in the privacy of darkness; closer than
Dara's courage would ever have allowed them to be. He
doesn't realise it, but this assistance in the search has
offered Ailbhe the most perfect of excuses: it allows her
to force a situation which she too has not had the
courage to create. Their faces are even closer to each
other now. They stoop a little further and, somewhere
between semi and full darkness, their cheeks touch.
Their faces flush and each is tempted to sit upright once
again, but, somehow, the darkness allows them to hold
the moment. The heat from each other's cheeks seems to
make the blood course even more quickly through their
veins. In the darkness they turn to face each other and,
as they do so, their noses touch. An accident of fate.
They feel a sensation – an excitement shoot through
them; a trembling in their lips. Again, the temptation is
to draw back, but now the will to stay as they are is even
greater. Dara purses his lips and, at the same time,
Ailbhe purses hers and both mouths meet. Her mouth,
her lips – as lovely and luscious, as he had imagined.
And Dara's mouth, his lips – lovely and luscious to her
too, just as she too had imagined. And they kiss. A kiss

of innocence, short and pure, and then their noses rest against each other for several seconds.

Then both come back up from the darkness and sit upright, their eyes fixed firmly on the screen before them. Dara pushes himself hard against the back of the seat and feels his heart racing in his chest, though he is trying to control it with his breathing. His effort is in vain. That kiss, though short, though pure, was far more than a mother's kiss. He can still taste it on his lips, and he tries to savour every single ounce of it. Is it the same for Ailbhe, he wonders. He is afraid to look in her direction to see what her reaction is. But he can still feel her hand in his and, unless he is misreading things, she is holding him even more tightly now. His heartbeat slows a little and he turns towards her. She is still looking towards the screen. His eyes focus on her lips again. Lovely luscious lips that now seem even redder than they were before. Then Ailbhe turns towards him and a gentle smile creeps across her lips. Both faces draw towards each other and, for a second time, they taste each other's lips.

—◇—

Dara walks quite briskly as he heads for home after leaving Ailbhe to her gate. This is a big night for him. He feels so happy that he wants to roar and shout and tell the world just what it's like to have been kissed. He can still taste their last kiss as they parted at the gate – still fresh, still strong, still dancing magically on his lips. And Brian Heffernan and the others in the school: well, what about them? Why bother? A shut mouth catches no flies, he thinks. He'll leave them to their talk . . .

52

INDISCRETION

Out of work. Idle. Unemployed. No matter what label was put on it, it all boiled down to the one thing in the end: John Connolly, like so many others, was condemned to standing in the dole queue every Thursday morning to collect the pittance of a handout the State would give him.

It was twenty-two months since the factory had closed down. Of course, at the time of closure, there were promises aplenty that it would reopen in a matter of months; the IDA were, supposedly, heavily engaged in discussions with a number of interested parties. It certainly wouldn't take any longer than three months to finalise a deal, they said. That proved to be nothing more than wishful thinking. Three months slipped into six, then on into nine. In the interim the IDA had been phased out and FORBAIRT took on a major part of its responsibilities. At this point it was nearly two years since the closure and any reopening seemed as far away as ever. Twenty-two months! The place would be gone to rack and ruin by the time they'd get around to doing anything with it.

John took the small army of coins from his pocket and counted them again. One pound, fifty-three pence. Holy Mother of God – not even the price of a pint. What possessed him at all that he didn't think of putting some of the money aside in the early stages when he was on the higher rate? He didn't know himself with all he had that first six months after the factory had closed. But then the drop came and with it, at pretty much the same time, the realisation that there was very little substance to the discussion the IDA or FORBAIRT, or anybody else may have been having. It all more or less amounted to the same thing. Talk, talk and more talk and not one whit of a result to it. Talk doesn't put food on the table or shoes on the children. It certainly doesn't pay the outstanding electricity bill.

John's mind began to wander, he had been so long standing in the queue. If he had it all to do over again he wouldn't go next or near the factory. Gardening. That's what he would have preferred by a long shot. Yes, indeed, gardening would have been his very first choice. He had had the chance to do it once, shortly before he started in the factory, but he didn't have the sense to take the opportunity when it presented itself. It was money ruled his mind at the time. He could make almost twice as much a week in the factory. Twelve years of soldering electronic circuit boards for computers that would be shifted halfway across the world. And what had he got to show for it in the end? Unemployment. Poverty. Nothing but anguish and the worry of where the next bite to eat might come from.

"How's it goin' there, Johnny?"

It was one of his former workmates. John knew it without even looking. It was only in the factory that anyone called him Johnny; it was there, in fact, that he had got the name. He turned. It was Billy Maguire, the man in charge of stores before the factory closed down. John's immediate feeling was that he would have much preferred not to have bumped into him at all. Billy was not exactly the type of person with whom John would normally associate; he was the sort that always had some scam or other on the go. If even half of what was said of him was true he was as crooked as a country lane.

"Ah, hello Billy," said John. He never had the gumption to let Billy know how little he thought of him. "Fairly badly," said John, in answer to Billy's initial question.

"Aw no, man," said Billy, and he made a strange Elvis-like gyration of the shoulders as he said it. Indeed, Elvis had been his nickname in the factory for that very reason. That and the hairstyle and the type of clobber he used to wear. Now that John looked at him, it was quite apparent that very little had changed. There he was before him, dressed impeccably: a pink-coloured tailored jacket, white shirt and grey trousers that had the slightest fleck of pink through them here and there. The only difference between the black well-groomed hair and the garish patent leather shoes was the leather. Huh, Elvis to a T, if ever he had seen him.

"Where's the action these days, my man?" asked Billy. Really, what he spoke could not be termed English. He had this habit of dotting everything he'd say with these Americanisms – not, however, the sort that Elvis would ever use at all, but a different type of terminology: things like *Man, Action, Dude, Cool, Awesome, What's goin' down? Get my drift?*

John laughed – a nervous laugh. "'Action' these days, Billy, is scarce to none to tell you the truth. There isn't an hour's work to be picked up anywhere."

"Work, man! Work! Don't mention that dirty word to me," said Billy. "Work and I have taken a holiday from each other – like, I mean lo-o-o-ong-term, man. Get my drift? Hell, there's better ways to get the greenbacks in than spilling sweat and tears, man."

John found Billy's language and his slimey way of going on quite revolting, but once again he found that he didn't have whatever it would take to let him know that. He simply smiled at Billy once again.

"Yeah, man, lots of different ways," said Billy.

Except for the fact that one does occasionally come across this type, one might be excused for thinking that Billy, or Elvis, as he preferred to regard himself, was one of these zany characters out of a cartoon or comic strip. He was smooth and smarmy and constantly trying to impress in a way that most people would tend to find repulsive.

"What do you mean? What are you on about?" asked John.

Billy looked around him in the dole queue. "Look, man," he said, "it's impossible to talk here. When you collect your money drop in next door to Bewley's and we'll discuss it over a cup of coffee."

"Johnny, Johnny, my man," came the shout as John

entered Bewley's. John turned in the direction of the shout, scanned the area, then spotted Billy.

"Over here, man."

They chit-chatted for a short while but then Billy turned on to the heavy stuff. There was something he wanted to discuss with John, he said.

"Look, man, see these threads, huh?" he said, as he slid his thumbs in under the lapels of his pink jacket. "Clobber like this doesn't grow on trees, you know. Twig, man? Do you get me? You need spondulicks to get into these – *smackarullahs,* man! And I'll tell you this, Johnny baby, I have the inside track on making the readies on a regular basis. Twig? Interested, huh? How about it, huh?"

John, of course, was more than a little interested in picking up any few quid he could, but he suspected that anything Billy might have afoot might be very much on the shady side. But then, for many reasons – lack of confidence, money pressures, idleness – John allowed Billy to develop the discussion even further.

Billy gave him the low-down on how he was pulling in the money – he and two others. Theft – that was the long and the short of it. It seemed that they had done all sorts since the factory had closed: houses, shops, cars, the lot.

"You name it, Johnny man, we've done it. Money for old rope, Johnny baby. Two sunshine holidays in the last ten months. A new car. Videos. You call it, man, we have it."

John was gripped by the conversation – afraid on the one hand of what he might hear, and yet, on the other hand, equally afraid to get up and leave. And the longer he stayed, the more Billy piled it on. "A nice little number in the offing," he told him. And there was room for a fourth man in the operation.

"And I'll tell you this, man, you'd do this one in your sleep. A piece of cake if ever there was one, Johnny boy. You're in if you want it."

John shook his head. No, he couldn't. There was his wife and his little son to be considered here. No, he just couldn't do it.

"Fair enough, my man," said Billy, "it's all down to yourself, but I'll tell you this: a blind man could carry this one off without a hitch."

But, despite John's rejection of the offer, Billy could discern that little glimmer of interest in his eyes. He'd press the matter a little.

"Look, Johnny, it's all the one to me whether you go with it or not, but just hear me out on this," he said.

Billy went on, explaining to John how this particular job was at the factory where they had worked.

"Remember, man, I was in charge of stores there. I know that building like the back of my hand, better than anybody else," said Billy. He had learned that all the stock, hundreds of personal computers were still stored there since the closure. But they were going to be shipped to the European plant very shortly, within a fortnight, his source had told him. And John knew that one thing was for certain: there really was no one who knew the ins and outs of that plant as well as Billy did.

"In, out and away with the goodies," said Billy. And then he looked at Johnny. For a fleeting moment it seemed to John that maybe Billy had it right. Afterall, John had been a hard and loyal worker for the company over the years. He certainly had never done anything to cause them to close up shop and leave him jobless. Billy could see a softening in John's eyes and he knew how best to play it.

"Listen, Johnny baby, I'm not going to put any pressure on you to do anything you don't want to do. It's your decision. The job's going down on Saturday night – the day after tomorrow. All we need is a driver, that's all. Myself and the other two will do the business. All you have to do is drive the van. There's an in for you, Johnny man, if you want it, but I have to have an answer by tomorrow. Fifty grand a man, minimum: £50,000! Piece of cake, Johnny, but it's up to yourself. Tomorrow at the latest. I'll be here again at one o'clock tomorrow, if you want to see me."

And with that Billy was gone. John raised his cup of coffee and could see his hand shake quite noticeably. It was as though the whole conversation had been a dream to him. The notion that he might even fleetingly have thought of rowing in with Billy sent a shiver through him. He threw back the coffee, sighed and decided to himself that, whatever else, this was something with which he would have no truck. He'd head on home to Aoife.

It's funny, but as John approached the front door of his house that day, he got the strangest feeling that something was badly wrong. His wife was seated at the kitchen table, in floods of tears, as he came in. She had a letter sqeezed tightly in her left hand.

"Aoife, love," he said, as he came towards her and then knelt beside her. He drew her head towards him and they pressed their faces against each other, forehead to forehead, nose to nose. "What is it, love?" he asked.

It was the worst of bad news. They had half-expected it for some time, but now that it had come, it was far worse than ever they could have anticipated. The house. The building society. They were nine months in arrears on their mortgage payments. Repossession was the only option now, the letter stated. What would they do? Where could they go? It seemed that there was nothing they could do.

With constant tossing and turning, John hardly slept a wink that night. At one point, just when he was finally about to nod off, he let a violent jump and awoke fully once again. His forehead was cold with sweat and, for a moment, he could see Billy Maguire's face in front of him. Yes, that was it. That's what he would do. Billy!

◄o►

Saturday night. A crystal-clear sky. John seated high up in the cab of the van and the back doors wide open, waiting for the loading. His mind was lost somewhere between the vast spread of stars overhead and thoughts of what £50,000 could do for him, for Aoife and for their little boy, Ian. They could keep the house at least. Indeed, they could buy it outright if that was what they decided upon. John would come up with some way of explaining the money to Aoife. The National Lottery, maybe, or the horses. Yes, the horses were a safer bet. More foolproof, really.

Billy and the other two were inside loading up the pallets. But what was keeping them? Billy had said it would take an hour max, but they were already in there one and three-quarter hours. Maybe there was a problem with a door, or with one of the pallet trucks. He thought of Billy and his "piece of cake". "Piece of cake, man". He found him repulsive, really. Even more repulsive to him was the fact that he found himself having to get involved with him in this way; that the system was so rotten, so inequitable that his only option, if he was to save family and home, was to get embroiled in the racketeering of a sleeveen like Billy Maguire.

Just then, John's mind was distracted by a beam of torchlight which caught his eye in the wing mirror of the van. They were some way in the distance to the rear. Two torches, in fact. What, in the name of God, was Billy at at all? There wasn't any need for torches on so clear a night. He opened the van door and jumped out, ready to shout at them to kill the lights. No sooner done than cruel reality hit home once again.

"All right, you, stay where you are. Gardaí – Special Crime Squad. Hands on the side of the van and spread your legs and arms."

Well, damn it, thought John.

The gardaí closed in then and, before John could come to terms with what was happening, one of them frisked him up and down his arms and legs. Then more gardaí arrived on the scene with Billy and his two sidekicks in tow.

"Keep a button on it, Johnny, man," shouted Billy to him. "Tell them nothing. Have you got that? Nothing. Zilch. You're entitled to a solicitor, man. Do you hear me? Ask to see your solicitor. Don't tell them anything unless he's present. Are you with me, Johnny, man? And you don't . . . "

Whatever final jewel of wisdom Billy was about to impart was drowned as he was bundled into one of the garda cars which had arrived on the scene. The rest of them were then put into a second car and whisked away for questioning.

The night became one long session of question after question in the garda station, each one of the four being questioned individually in separate interrogation rooms.

"Remember your wife and child, Connolly," one of the detectives half-threateningly said to John. And John, of course, did. Indeed, they were what totally consumed his mind.

"You play ball with us and things will be a lot easier for you, John," a second detective advised. And John played ball.

Yes, indeed, John played ball in every way possible. He spilled out his own story, chapter and verse, holding nothing back: how tough things were, how his confidence had waned, how they were in danger of losing the house. The whole lot, sparing absolutely nothing. Anyway, as things turned out, the gardaí knew that, up to now, John had had nothing to do with this outfit. It became apparent that they had had them under surveillance for quite some time. But, nonetheless, there was no getting away from the fact that John had been a part of this particular operation. No less than the others, he would have to go to court, but the gardaí promised, given his cooperation, that they would make a case for him.

Some months later, in court, the gardaí gave their account of things. To give them their due, they made it very clear that there was, in their opinion, a discernible difference between the cases of John Connolly and those of the other three defendants. They made as good a case for him as they could, so good in fact that the judge invited John to expound somewhat on his circumstances.

John felt that he had got an understanding hearing and he was quite hopeful of the judge's decision in the end. There was no doubt where the other three were concerned that a prison sentence would be handed down, but John's own solicitor had intimated to him that he felt he would get less than that. Community service of one sort or another was more likely in his case. That would serve the purpose well on all fronts – both the community at large and John himself. It would also boost his own self-esteem and confidence and one never knew – it might even offer an opportunity to earn an extra few bob on top of the dole. It's an ill wind, indeed, thought John to himself.

The other three were badly rocked when the court's decision was announced. It wasn't so much that they hadn't expected it, but more the case that when something is finally and definitively announced, it hits home in a way that a mere expectation cannot do. Billy Maguire went down for eight years; the other two for five years each. That was pretty much along the lines expected. All three looked stony-faced as John's sentence was awaited.

John could not be sure that he had heard correctly when finally the judge delivered his decision. Whatever about the sentences for the other three hitting hard, John was absolutely stunned when the judge made his pronouncement. He could not believe it. Three years in prison. Three years! After all that his solicitor had said about thinking he might only get a stint doing community service. His first inclination was to laugh: nervous laughter. But that inclination was quickly dispelled by the long shrill sound of Aoife crying in the body of the courthouse. My God, three years. John turned and looked back at Aoife, now in a slumped and sorry state behind him. And, beside her, little Ian, totally bemused at what had occasioned his mother to burst out in tears like this. Ian would be eight, almost nine years of age by the time his father would be released from prison. No John there to slip the money under the pillow when his son's first tooth fell out; no John, either, to stand with him when he made his First Communion. All those special little moments in a child's life now gone for John.

Every single day in prison seemed more like three days to John Connolly: one for his lovely wife, Aoife, one for his little boy, and the third – that which he was due to serve by right. He worked the hoe against the clay at the stem of one of the saplings in the prison garden and stooped to pick up a bright silver coin which he had unearthed. It was a one-pound coin, clear and shiny on front, but, on the back, clay had embedded itself in the narrow crevices between the harp strings. John ran the nail of his forefinger between the strings in an effort to clean the coin. He looked then at his forefinger and saw the self-same dirt embedded beneath the fingernail. Somehow he felt that this coin which he had found was his by right. It wasn't £50,000 or anything like it, but at least it was rightfully his. When Aoife and Ian would come to visit him on Friday he would squeeze it into his little boy's hand. He rain his thumb along the the body of the stag on the front face of the coin and slipped the one-pound piece into his prison tunic.

ADRIFT

My thoughts today, though I'm far away,
Dwell on Tír Chonaill's shore,
The salt sea air and the colleens fair
Of lovely green Gweedore;
There's a colleen there beyond compare
That I'll treasure evermore,
She's a grand colleen in her gown of green,
She's the . . .

"Hello. Are you there, Bridie? Hello, Bridie, it's me – Deirdre."

As soon as Bridie heard Deirdre's voice she stopped singing. She slipped the bottle of meths down inside the separated cardboard box which served as a blanket to her and straightened herself a little before Deirdre made her way in.

"How are you doing tonight then, Bridie?" the young woman asked, as she entered the dilapidated shed that, for all intents and purposes, was home to Bridie Bonner for the past three weeks or so. She was fortunate to have got so long out of the one place. More often than not, one would be hounded out of a place within the first week.

To look at her, one would put Bridie Bonner at sixty years of age, at least, maybe even seventy. Bridie Bonner, or Bridie Doherty-Bonner, as she herself used to say at one time. She was a Doherty from the Rosses originally but had been in Dublin since some time in the mid-sixties. That's where she met her first and only love, Liam. He worked in the Department of Finance at the time – one of those diligent, conscientious civil servants whose future was assured and for whom the steady climb up the promotional ladder was in prospect. Within a year of meeting one another they were married. Before another year had passed their first child, Liam Óg, was born. And then, in 1969, the second of their children had arrived: a beautiful little baby girl, called Saoirse. The name had been chosen because of the festering troubles in the North at the time. Little did Bridie think that, by the time the late seventies would come around, she would have considerable troubles of her own.

It was the first day of December 1979 that Liam walked in and announced baldly that he had contracted cancer of the lungs. Cigarettes, it was suspected, had done the major part of the damage or, if such was not the case, they most certainly had not helped the situation. Despite the bad news, Liam was positive in his attitude. They would fight the illness together. "A united family" was their motto at the time. A united family. Little did they realise what a weakened united family they would become within the next two years. November 1981 – poor old Liam didn't even get to ring in the New Year.

"I've lovely thick soup for you tonight, Bridie," said Deirdre, coming closer to her. "Full of wholesome vegetables and piping hot."

Bridie took the bowl from her and started right into it. It was the first thing she had tasted since Deirdre had been with her the previous night. Were it not for the fact that it was so hot it would have been gone in a jiffy.

"Mmm, tasty! Lovely and tasty," said Bridie, and she looked over the rim of the bowl at Deirdre. There was a hint of distraction in her eyes, eyes that were for all the world like a badger's when he's backed against a wall. Then Bridie smiled across at the younger woman.

"God bless you, Deirdre, love. You're very good to me. You'll get your reward in Heaven and that's for sure." And with that she tucked into what remained in the bowl.

"Take it easy, Bridie, take it easy. There's no hurry. The night is long."

Deirdre was a young Dubliner, just finished her third year in Trinity College. Given the employment situation at home, the signs were that, within a year or so, she might have to give up the SIMON soup run and head across the water or to the States, maybe.

"Your son is abroad, Bridie, isn't he?"

Bridie nodded, then reached her hand towards the tea and sandwiches which Deirdre had arranged before her.

"Where is he, Bridie? What country?

"Canada," said Bridie, but beyond that she showed no interest in offering detail.

"Canada is a big country, Bridie. Whereabouts in Canada is he?"

"Well now, you may as well be asking that wall over there. I've no more a clue than yourself," she said and, as she spoke, Deirdre could see the tears welling in her eyes and there was a tremble in her voice which was not there before. Then Bridie lowered her head and allowed the tears to fall.

Deirdre remained silent until Bridie chose to speak again, and when she did, it was of her son in Canada that she spoke. She told of how, despite great difficulty, she had managed to keep the show on the road until after Liam Óg and Saoirse had graduated from university. That in itself was quite an achievement considering that, being so young when he died, Liam's pension had been very small and Bridie had been obliged to do housework to keep things ticking over until the children had finished their studies.

It was drink that tore the family asunder in the end, she said. She had never fully got her act together after Liam had died. All that love so cruelly taken from her was far too much for her to handle. She had managed to keep her drinking habit a secret from the children for quite some time. It was only as Saoirse was nearing her finals that she and Liam began to notice things not being right; only then did they realise that Bridie's drinking had been going on for quite some time and that she was so fully in the grips of it that something urgently needed to be done. But Bridie rejected all approaches. She didn't have the energy to face coming to terms with her problem. All she wanted was that which was impossible for her to have: her own loving Liam back with her. But one thing was for certain – if she kept going the way she was, it wouldn't be very long before they would see each other once again.

The drinking got worse and, as it did, the gap widened between herself and the children. Liam Óg took himself off to Canada and that was the last Bridie had ever heard of him. Gone. Her own son for whom she had worked her fingers to the bone to ensure that he got every possible opportunity in life. And Saoirse, her daughter: she lived in Bray now, as far as Bridie knew. She had married a solicitor and, to Bridie's knowledge, they had just the two children – a boy and a girl, just like herself and Liam had had.

"Where in Bray does she live, Bridie?" asked Deirdre. She had resisted the temptation to interrupt her up to now, feeling somehow that it was good for Bridie to get all she had to say out into the open.

"God bless us, Deirdre, love, but sure I haven't got the foggiest notion." She looked into Deirdre's eyes as she spoke and the younger woman thought that she could see some little element of hope rekindled in Bridie Bonner's eyes.

"And do you know what her married name is?" asked Deirdre, thinking that it might be possible to locate the daughter's name in the telephone directory and maybe even bring them together again, if that's what they both wanted. Deirdre was not too sure whether to mention this idea to Bridie or not, or whether it would be best to leave things as they were.

"Would you like, Bridie, if I were to try to locate your daughter and maybe even see about the two of you getting together again?"

Suddenly, Bridie burst into floods of tears. This time the crying was long and heavy and Deirdre decided it was best to let it run its course.

"Saoirse and Michael Coyne," volunteered Bridie when she had finished crying.

"And would you like to meet her again, Bridie?" asked Deirdre for a second time. Bridie shook her head vigorously and blurted tearfully.

"No. No, I wouldn't," she said. "I'd just like to see the house – see where she lives with my little grandchildren. That's all, that's all." And the tears took over once again. Again, Deirdre let her cry and, when finally the tears had abated, she asked:

"Would you like to come out with me on the DART from Dún Laoghaire tomorrow, Bridie? It's a lovely trip to Bray. I could look up your daughter's address in the telephone directory, and we could go and look at the house – no need to do any more than that if that's what you want. What do you think, Bridie?"

Bridie raised her head again and Deirdre could see the light of the lamp which she had brought with her on her rounds dance in the old woman's eyes. Her face was filled with a mixture of hope and happiness and, as she looked at her, Deirdre realised for the first time ever how beautiful this gentle woman was.

"Yes, I would like that. I would like that very much," said Bridie, and she squeezed the young woman's hand in gratitude.

–◇–

It was ten to twelve next morning and Bridie had still not arrived at Dún Laoghaire DART station. She was an hour late already. Deirdre looked at the station clock, then up and down the platform once again. She wasn't coming. Deirdre thought that she should, perhaps, go up to the back of the old garage on Mulgrave Street and see if Bridie was still there. Then she thought better of that – it was best not to. Maybe the old lady had had a change of heart and, if that was the case, Deirdre could do more harm than good going up and appearing to pressurise her into doing something which she had decided against. Anyway, she'd get to see her later on that night.

There was no singing to be heard as Deirdre neared Bridie's shed later on that night. No *Rose of Aranmore* or any other music. Nothing but the scratching of a rat's nail beneath the separated cardboard box where Bridie Doherty-Bonner lay dead beside her bottle of methylated spirits.

LEGACY

*To the memory of Veronique Mernier, who finally
lost her battle with AIDS in January 1991.*

He lay on his back and stared at the ceiling. Its jade
green colour was gentle on his eyes, despite the general
discomfort he felt lying in the hospice for the dying. A
kindly colour. He was surprised that he had come to like
it; it was a colour that, just a few years ago, he had
detested. Strange, he thought, how in a time of crisis,
one can change one's view of things; how one can come
to like something when it is in danger of being taken
away. And, by now, of course, one thing was for sure, it
would be taken from him; the jade, white, yellow, red,
every single colour that ever he had seen. All gone with
death. Three months, maybe, three weeks, three days . . .
they couldn't say for certain. The only certainty was that
it would happen sooner or later.

Faces visited themselves on him from time to time,
their coming very much dependent on his frame of
mind: Rock Hudson, Magic Johnson, Freddie Mercury,
Arthur Ashe. All big names, big people; people who had
made their mark in life in one way or another; people

whose names were household names the world over. But where did that leave him, Éamonn Kelly, who had not done one iota of consequence in this world? Why him? At nineteen years of age. What message, what wisdom, what advice could he ever possibly have to leave to this world? What warning could he offer about the state in which he found himself? About his illness? And who would bother with anything that he might have to say?

He fingered the silver Claddagh ring on his index finger, then rubbed it with his thumb. He could feel the crevices of the design, the fingers and the outline of the heart, with his thumbnail. The rubbing soothed his mind back to the day the ring had been stolen, the day of the break-in on the jeweller's shop.

It had never been intended that anyone would be injured. In fact, they were quite determined that such would not be the case: in and out, make the grab and leave the staff of the place tied up in the storeroom. So much for theory.

It was a theory that backfired; a theory that denied the practicalities of reality. What, in the name of God, had possessed the owner that he tried to stop them? Why couldn't he simply have let things take their course, as planned? He could have done the simple thing and gone into the storeroom with the rest of his staff. Then everything would have been fine. It certainly hadn't figured in their thinking that he might try to take them on. That wasn't part of the plan.

Éamonn could still see the owner's face. It hadn't been part of the plan either that he'd be stabbed. It was an impulsive reaction to the tension of the situation. The change in the owner's face as soon as the knife made contact – the open mouth, the bulging eyes, the colour of his face changing from red to a sickly grey. He hadn't reckoned on that at all. And then the blood. The owner's blood. Even now, in bed, Éamonn rubbed his hands together, trying to wipe away the memory of the blood. The redness of the blood; the cleanness of it. Cleanness! Much cleaner than his own blood at this point of the game. Strong, clean, unpolluted blood.

"Éamonn, Éamonn, your mother rang to say she'll be in in a while, but she'll be a little late today."

The nurse's voice broke Éamonn's train of thought. He raised his head a little and looked towards the doorway where she was standing.

"Your mother, Éamonn. She'll be in later."

Éamonn shook his head ever so slightly. The nurse knew it was his way of saying thanks. Speech was very difficult for him at this stage; hard on the windpipe, painful. Nonetheless, he loved to have visitors come – his only link with the outside world. And even if he did find speech painful now, his hearing was still very much intact. Yes, he loved his mother's visits, looked forward to them, relied on them. This was so different to the time he had done in Saint Patrick's Institution.

Saint Patrick's! A one-year sentence when he was only sixteen. Two visits per week was the limit there. And then they found out he was HIV positive and he didn't want to see anyone who might come to visit him. But fair dues to his mother. A marvellous woman. She just kept coming, even at times when he would refuse to see her.

That was all of three years ago now. But even at this stage, with full-blown AIDS rampant throughout his body, he had time to think of how great his mother had been to him. There wasn't one single day that she hadn't come. There was a world of difference between the hospice and the prison. She would stay with him for hours each day. Indeed, sometimes she would even come twice, morning and afternoon, and just sit and talk and touch. Loyalty. Love.

Love. The Claddagh ring. Again he felt the contours of the heart with his thumbnail. Love. It was a lovely idea, he thought: the heart protected in the warmth of the hands; the safety of the hands; mothering hands.

It seemed odd to him that his only worry in the world now was this feeling that he didn't have anything of value to leave behind him. Nothing material, no wisdom, no nothing. Nothing to do but wait. From time to time other questions of huge import would enter his mind; questions with which he could not contend, coming from God knows where. He'd simply let them slip away again, refusing to allow them to create any turmoil in his mind.

But this question of what he might leave behind . . . What advice? What wisdom? He knew that this was one which he was capable of figuring out. It was important to him that he do so. Then the faces came visiting again. Mercury, Johnson, Hudson, Ashe. It was as though they were on a rôtisserie of some sort, turning, smiling, inviting him to join them; asking him to add whatever his message to the world might be to theirs. He turned it over in his mind again: they had sport or music or some particular achievement on which to base any message they might choose to give. But he – Éamonn Kelly – he had nothing. Nothing at all, he felt. He closed his mind to the faces now, but he knew that they would be back again in a while.

His mind was easy now: no thoughts, no turmoil, not even the ghosting in and out of faces to bother him now. The green jade ceiling once again. The gentleness of the colour on his eyes. It was like balsam to him now after the barrage of thought. Silence. But silence, like all things, tires of itself in time. He'd welcome a little turmoil now – even the mental turmoil of before. What advice? What message could he leave? And even if it came to him, would he have the ability to pass it on? How would he pass it on? He scratched the ring frantically with his fingernail: he could feel the heart, the hands, the crown on top. He felt quite close to understanding. A matter of time, a minute, a second . . .

Then, suddenly, his eyes widened. He had it. Yes. He reached his right hand back towards the headrest of the bed, located the cold, metal bars and grabbed hold of one towards the centre of the row. Then, bar by bar, he moved out until he located the thickest of the bars at the outside of the frame. He felt his way up along the thick bar until he reached the little bell, then pushed. Down with the hand again and he waited for the nurse to come. A half-minute, a minute, ten minutes passed, perhaps, before she came.

"Well, Éamonn, were you ringing?"

His look confirmed that he was.

"And what do you want, love?" she asked kindly. She

had bright, gentle eyes that Éamonn thought should surely have been jade in colour.

"What is it you need, Éamonn? Is it a drink?" It wasn't. "What is it then, Éamonn?"

Éamonn's lips were quivering. Even the thought of speaking was painful for him. He wanted to get what needed saying over and done with in one clean effort. The nurse could see him readying his lips for speech. She leaned forward and put her ear quite close to his mouth.

"Pp . . . ppp . . . pppp . . . " He stopped. The pain in his windpipe was excruciating. The nurse squeezed his shoulder gently and coiffed back the strands of hair that lay across his face. As she did so, she could feel the beads of sweat forming on his face.

"I'm sorry, Éamonn, love," she said. "Can you try one more time? Just one more little effort."

Éamonn squeezed his eyes shut, then opened again. The sparkle of intent was still there. He would give it another go. Again, the thought of speaking and the pain in his neck came at one and the same time. He kept telling himself that he would get it out, that he would not be beaten. His lips were trembling once again and the nurse waited, determined that, this time, she would catch whatever it was that he was trying to say.

"Pp . . . ppp . . . ppen and pp . . . " and again he had to give way to the pain. He closed his mouth and felt the windpipe tightening inside his neck. The nurse squeezed his shoulder a second time. "A pen, Éamonn, is it?" she asked.

He shook his head a little.

"A pen and something else, is it?" Again, a shake of the head. "What else, Éamonn? Paper, I suppose! Is it, Éamonn? Is it a pen and paper you want?"

Éamonn smiled broadly and his eyes filled with light. The nurse left and came back again in a jiffy, carrying with her a pen and a notebook. It dawned on her as she returned that there would be even greater effort required of Éamonn now; even greater pain. He did not have sufficient control of his faculties to write a single letter, never mind a word, or words. He would have to enunciate every single syllable for her. She drew closer to him once again and leaned forward.

"Now then, Éamonn, what is it you want to say?"

Éamonn braced himself yet again. The shudder in the lips, the glint of hopefulness in his eyes, the fingernails digging hard into the softness of the mattress. The previous effort had taken so much out of him. He raised his head from the pillow.

"Mes . . . mess . . . mess . . . " and he stopped and fell back again.

"A mess, is it, Éamonn? Something's in a mess. Is that it, Éamonn?" but no sooner had she asked him than she knew intuitively that that was not it.

Éamonn looked frustrated. All that effort and to no avail. The nurse was thinking hard, combing her mind to come up with some word that sounded like "mess". And then, it hit her:

"Message, is it, Éamonn? Is it 'message'?"

Again, that broad beam spread itself across his mouth. Yes, she had got it; she had got it at last, thank God for that.

78

"Message. Good Éamonn, good. And what is the message then, Éamonn?"

The broad beam on Éamonn's mouth narrowed itself back to normality and receded then to a look of frustration once again. How was he going to tell her that the word "message" was the actual message he wanted to impart? He wasn't sure that he could muster the energy required to make another effort.

"Can you tell me what the message is, Éamonn?" She was kind, gentle; it was breaking her heart to be so demanding of him. Again, ear to shuddering lips, a summoning of courage and . . .

"Mess . . . age," said Éamonn, and he fell back, exhausted, as he uttered the second syllable. He raised his hand to his windpipe and realised that he could give no more. The nurse too, realised that this was the case. She was uncertain whether or not to question him any further and to ask him simply to gesture towards one thing or another in a final effort to figure out what was of such importance to him.

"And, Éamonn, what is the message? Can you point? Can you show me with your eyes?"

Slowly, surely, Éamonn's eyes moved to meet those of this kindly nurse. From there he shifted his gaze to the piece of paper where she had written "message". Then her own eyes followed Éamonn's gaze on to the paper. She turned back towards him and their eyes met once again. For a second time, Éamonn deliberately lowered his eyes towards the piece of paper, again compelling the nurse to follow suit. Another look at each other and then, as though by telepathy, she understood that the word "message" was what constituted Éamonn's message.

"So, that's it, Éamonn! The word 'message' is the actual message you want to give, is it?"

He smiled yet again, finally confirming to the nurse that that was it. "Message."

She wrote it down afresh on a second sheet of paper and held it in front of Éamonn's eyes.

"Message," she said, quite boldly now, and she watched as the broad beaming smile returned to Éamonn's lips.

"So, what am I to do with it," asked the nurse, "now that we've finally managed to get it right?" Éamonn looked towards the little bedside locker.

"Put it on top of the bedside locker, is it, Éamonn?"

Again the smile, again the glint in Éamonn's eyes; eyes full of gratitude to her. He would sleep a little now, maybe, before his mother would come to visit.

It was near to three that afternoon when Éamonn's mother came to see him. Somehow, even before she came into the room, she had a premonition that Éamonn had finally found the peace that he was seeking; that pain and he had parted company at last. She pulled in by the bedside. His features were totally undrawn; his face at peace, angelic, whiter than the whiteness of the sheets; cold. And the smile was one of happiness. Happiness, at last, because now the suffering was over and he had finally succeeded in his effort to leave his little piece of wisdom – the message which he had striven so hard to formulate.

His mother looked over at the bedside locker and

there, on top, sat the bright silver Claddagh ring and, beneath it, the sheet of paper on which the nurse had written Éamonn's message to the world. The crown sat comfortably on the heart, and both sat warmly embraced in the security of the hands: all there as testimony to Éamonn Kelly's effort.

KIDNAP

"Times! *Lá breá*," says the newspaper vendor outside of Dún Laoghaire train station, trying out his little bit of Irish, as often he would do when he'd see Niamh approaching. Niamh hands him the eighty-five pence. By this stage they know each other quite well, though they rarely exchange any more than a half-dozen words. Some days prior to this he had asked Niamh what the Irish word for "change" is. "Sóinseáil", she had told him, but unfortunately for him, Niamh has had the exact change ready every morning since. You could tell to look at him that the poor devil was just dying to use the new word ever since he had been given it.

"There's the train," she says, as she feels the ground rumble beneath her feet. She shoves *The Irish Times* under her arm, scurries down the station steps and by the ticket checker, waving her monthly pass at him.

The DART on this particular morning is no different to any other: packed, black with people, loads of seats all right but, unfortunately, a backside well and truly planted on each and every one of them. Niamh stands on the sea-side of the carriage and, just before the train moves off again, grabs the chrome bar in front of her. The darkness of the sky these winter mornings casts its own particular beauty on the water. Here and there the sun forces its way through gaps in the heavy black clouds, casting little tints of silver on the water. Across the way, on the other side of the bay, the lighted streetlamps of Howth are still visible.

"Pardon me, I'm sorry," says the man alongside her. His hand has accidentally touched against Niamh's as he also grabs on to the chrome bar. She looks at him, grimaces a little, then focuses her eyes back on the metal bar. She takes stock of his hand now. It is covered in an expensive-looking brown leather glove. Again, she averts her eyes a little, this time resting them on his overcoat: it is a dark brown crombie – expensive also. Up a little and she sees a slouch hat – the same shade of brown as are the gloves, and around it a satin band identical in colour to the overcoat.

A sudden jerk and the train has come to a standstill. Niamh looks out towards the platform. Blackrock already! She hadn't even noticed the stops at Salthill or at Seapoint. Morningitis, she thinks, and rubs the sleep from her eyes.

The compartment is very full now. Niamh used to think that such congestion only happened in places like Tokyo and New York and other larger cities of the world. There is another man across from her now who is dressed almost identically to the first man. The only difference is that this man's attire is predominantly navy in colour, but the style is very much the same. There is the pleasant smell of musk from one of them but Niamh cannot quite figure which one is wearing it.

Booterstown. In the distance Ringsend power station stands boldly against the winter morning sky; then a row of houses blocks it from view. And then another stop: Sydney Parade. A small exodus from the train but as many again, if not more, come on board.

Sandymount . . . Lansdowne . . . Pearse Station: they pour out from the train and the sense of airiness inside the compartment now seems strange to Niamh. It's ironic, she thinks, how this relief of congestion always happens just when she is about to disembark. Tara Street – out she gets. A look at her watch: 8.25 am – loads of time. She'll have coffee, as usual, in the little bistro beside Liberty Hall.

Down the station steps. The big man dressed in brown who had been beside her on the DART is on the stairs in front of her. She feels impatient because she cannot see her way ahead of him. Though she doesn't realise it, the second man is behind her now. She has a strange feeling of uneasiness: trying to escape the discomfort she had sensed on the train and yet still feeling some restriction on her. She passes through the ticket collector's gate and suddenly the openness of the foyer and the prospect of the street ahead promises the relief that she has wanted. Thank God for that. Fresh air, light, room to breathe.

She stands on the edge of the path. The little red man at the pedestrian lights is looking over at her, cautioning her to stay where she is until he changes colour. Green now, and Niamh is just about to cross when she is suddenly grabbed by an elbow on either side and swept swiftly towards a large limousine-type car which has pulled up in the centre of the street. She is bundled in so quickly that she really hasn't got a grasp of all that is happening around her.

On the back seat of the car now, Niamh looks about her. A man on either side of her – the two who had been with her on the train. Two others, of similar dress and stature, sit up front. The two to the rear have so hemmed Niamh in that she doesn't have the leverage to move freely. All four men look straight ahead in silence. Niamh is confused. It's almost as if what is happening is somehow outside of her; as if she is an observer of something happening to somebody else. She is still trying to make sense of what is going on. Then, suddenly, reality registers with her. She screams . . .

"Let me out, let me out! I'm . . . "

A hand slips quickly across her shoulder and on to her mouth. A bitter taste of leather in her mouth that makes her nauseous and, for some seconds, there is a danger that she may throw up. Suddenly, the car surges forward. All Niamh can see is pedestrians scattering in all directions in an effort to avoid being hit. Through the lights on O'Connell Bridge, past the Virgin Megastore and on towards the open road and the West. A strong smell now pervades the car. It is not the pleasant scent of musk, but something stronger, much more pungent. Now she sees a second hand holding a white cloth reaching across to her . . . the smell strengthens and then closes in on her as the cloth is pressed firmly against her nose and, despite herself, Niamh is inhaling the noxious fumes. A grey cloud spreads itself across her mind, then turns to black.

◄○►

"Gardaí are still inquiring into the suspected abduction of Niamh Brennan, the young woman seen being swept into a car outside the Tara Street DART station yesterday morning. They are appealing to anyone who may have been in the vicinity of the station between 8.15 am and 8.35 am, and who may have seen the incident in question, to please make contact with them at Pearse Street Gar . . . "

"Turn off that bloody radio. We don't want her knowing anything about any of this," said one of the four kidnappers.

The door of the room where Niamh is being kept is a little ajar and, from where she's seated, Niamh can make out the shape of one of the kidnappers against the faint morning light which is creeping through the curtains on the kitchen window.

"Shush," the same man says. "She could waken any minute for all we know."

Indeed! If only he knew that Niamh had been sitting there awake for over an hour now, none of them would have said half as much as already had been said. She is still a little groggy and she can get the smell of chloroform where some had spilled down on her blouse. This quarter of a million pounds of which she heard the men speak some time earlier – she had her doubts that her stepfather could raise that for her. Indeed, her real doubt was whether or not he would be prepared to raise that, or anything else, for her. She could never understand what her mother had seen in him. He couldn't hold a candle to her father – a mild, gentle man. The only similarity between the two men was that they were both involved with financial institutions. Why couldn't the likes of him have died instead of her father, Niamh often wondered to herself.

The silence is intense now that the radio has been turned off. Gradually, Niamh's ear attunes itself to the morning chorus of the birds outside. Not a car or lorry or any semblance of traffic to be heard. There is the occasional lowing of a cow to be heard in the distance and, every now and then, the braying of a donkey. She must be somewhere down the country. She'd like to look out the window but being tied to the chair puts paid to that possibility. Thoughts of the rope draws her attention to the soreness of her wrists. It would be nice if she could loosen the rope just a little. A scream might get her some attention but then she thinks twice on that. It might only alarm her captors and would probably result in another dose of chloroform. Suddenly, she is distracted by the sound of a car pulling up outside. The sound of heavy wheels grinding their tyres hard against the gravel. A door opening and closing. The strange whirring of an engine after it has been turned off. Footsteps coming towards the house – leather-soled shoes – thinks Niamh: she can distinguish the difference between leather and rubber against the gravel chippings. A coded knock on the outside door and the stranger enters. Niamh finds it difficult to make full sense of anything that's said outside in the kitchen, but she does manage to pick up the odd word here and there.

"The back room", "asleep", "hasn't a clue", "insurance" are amongst the few discernible words she hears.

Niamh tries to move her chair over towards the door. As she moves, the legs of the chair screech sharply against the stone tiles on the floor. She stops. Outside in the kitchen the talk has also stopped. She hears footsteps coming towards the door. The door is pushed more widely open and there, standing against the jamb, is one of the kidnappers. Niamh keeps her eyes focused on the ground beneath her. The kidnapper backs away again and closes the door behind him. As the door is drawn, Niamh raises her head and catches a glimpse of the wine-coloured briefcase outside on the kitchen floor: gold metal capping on each corner to protect it from being scuffed and damaged. The door is closed. Darkness. The talk in the kitchen seems quite distant now. After a while she can hear the footsteps on the gravel once again. The starting of the car, reversing, then leaving.

The radio in the kitchen now. News headlines once again:

"Gardaí have announced that the young woman abducted outside Tara Street station early yesterday morning is Niamh Brennan. Niamh is a daughter of the deceased banker, Mr Ultan Brennan, and his widow, Sheila. She is the stepdaughter of the international financial consultant, Mr Raymond Proctor. The Garda Information Office has confirmed in the last half-hour that a ransom note demanding one quarter of a million pounds has been received by Mr Proctor.

The statement this morning by the leader of the SDLP, Mr . . . "

Days pass, Niamh cannot be sure how many: three, four, maybe even five. She is still confined to the back room off the kitchen, her only relief being mealtimes and visits to the toilet. She has very little contact with her captors other than being told, from time to time, that things are going to plan and that they think she will be released before too long. But she cannot be sure of that. She is doubting everything; recalling similar cases where the money had not been paid. What would happen if the money was not paid? Would they torture her? Maybe even worse.

The night of the sixth or seventh day – Niamh does not know which for sure. Headlights sweep across the curtains and fill the room. Yet again, the weight of tyres grinding against the gravel and then that whirring sound of the engine settling itself. The heavy drone of talk in the kitchen once again: too heavy, too deep to be able to figure out what's being said. The click of briefcase latches . . . the wine-coloured briefcase, Niamh supposes. More talk and then the visitor leaves again. And quietness settles back around her.

At some point in the middle of the night Niamh hears the creaking of the door into her room. A shaft of light makes its way in through the opening and, in its wake, two of her captors enter. She senses danger and her immediate impulse is to scream, but she cannot do so – the gag put across her mouth earlier in the night has seen to that; the very effort to scream has hurt her. Before she even thinks of crying in pain, the kidnappers have grabbed her. Now she can smell the chloroform again.

Niamh tries to fight them off but the effort is futile. One of the men rips the adhesive gag from her mouth, then presses the saturated cloth against her nose. Niamh's eyes roll back into her head and the yellow light dances in them, then fades to dark.

When Niamh awakens the doctor is by her bedside. She recognises her surroundings – she is in her own bedroom at home. Her mother and stepfather are by the bedside too. Peace and quiet is advised before she speaks to the gardaí. The doctor's advice is that any reading of newspapers is totally out of the question for at least the next few days.

In time Niamh assists the gardaí in any way she can, though what she can tell them seems quite insignificant. Apart from the detail of how the men were dressed, there is very little else that she can tell them. She is informed that the £250,000 demanded by the kidnappers has been paid. Most fortunately, as it transpires, her stepfather has insured himself, Niamh's mother and Niamh herself against just such an eventuality – a practice that nowadays, it seems, is commonplace in the world of international finance. Such people set easy targets for the kidnapper. And, given the urgency of demand and, most probably, Raymond Proctor's standing in the scheme of things, the insurance company has been quick in coming forward with the money. Niamh feels that she has, perhaps, been far too critical of her stepfather.

◄o►

A fine springlike day in late February. It's been six full weeks since Niamh's unfortunate ordeal. Saturday morning. Niamh is lying back on the sitting-room settee, totally absorbed in the latest copy of *Hello* magazine. Her mother is fussing about, looking for her handbag, while her stepfather is taking the car out of the garage. Niamh is engrossed in an article on the trials of George Michael's battle with his recording company, Sony International, when she hears her stepfather's Saab pull up in front of the house. He stops the engine – then a strange whirring sound is heard.

Niamh's eyes widen in fear and her body seems to freeze. She can feel her limbs tremble now. Slowly, she eases her head above the back of the settee and sees her mother get into the passenger seat of the car. The engine is restarted and the Saab heads out towards the front gate. Niamh is rigid with fear: the whirring of the engine is still ringing in her ears; she is afraid to turn around lest there be someone behind her. Memories of being confined in darkness come flooding back to her now; she even thinks that she can catch the smell of chloroform. No, she can't . . . she can't, she tells herself.

Niamh lies still on the settee for quite some time, thought after thought coursing through her mind. Car lights in the dark . . . the grinding of gravel . . . the whirring of an engine . . . the crunching sound of leather soles against stone chippings . . . a coded knock on a door . . . muffled words outside in a kitchen . . . gold-coloured capping on a briefcase. The briefcase . . . the briefcase! Niamh's eyes widen once again and her heart begins to race. The briefcase!

She steels her courage now and turns around on the settee: there is no one behind her. She stands and moves out to the hall, up the stairs and into her mother and stepfather's bedroom. She heads towards the walk-in closet where she knows there is a collection of travelbags and the like. She grabs the door handle, then stops. Should she really do this? she wonders. Perhaps it would be better to leave things as they are. But the memory of the chloroform comes to mind again and, instinctively, she turns the handle.

There are bags of all descriptions inside in the closet, from travelbags to shopping bags to all sorts else. A plethora of briefcases that had belonged to her father and as many again of Raymond Proctor's; they are piled there, one on top of the other. She puts her hand on top of the pile and slowly moves down, case by case: grey, black, brown, tan . . . suddenly, she hears the whirring of the car engine outside again. She rushes to the window. My God – her stepfather! He's on his own. What in the name of God is he doing back so soon? Niamh rushes back to the closet door and slams it shut. Her heart is thumping hard against her ribcage. The hall door below opens now and she hears Raymond Proctor calling.

"It's only me, Niamh. I left my wallet by the bed." His talk has been directed towards the sitting-room, where he presumes Niamh is still reading.

Already Niamh is on the phone in the upstairs bedroom. She has dialled 999 and has already given her name and address. Her heart is thumping even harder now. Proctor is halfway up the stairs by now, coming near the landing when Niamh opens the bedroom door.

They both stop and look at each other, Niamh's eyes filled with fear; his eyes hard and cold. Niamh feels her body go rigid as she looks at him.

"Niamh!" he says.

He looks despicable to Niamh. Worse again, however, he looks dangerous.

Suddenly, he moves on to the landing but, as he does so, Niamh quickly backs into the bedroom and slams the door shut. She manages to turn the key in the lock before Proctor reaches the door.

"Niamh," he says, trying to sound half-reasonable. Niamh backs away from the door now, her eyes fixed on the turning handle.

"Niamh," he says again, and this time the turning of the handle is somewhat more frenetic.

Niamh is back on the phone, her eyes alternating between the turning of the doorhandle and the dialling of the nines. She is saturated with sweat – even her fingertips, she notices. The turning of the doorhandle is violent now and Proctor rams his shoulder against the outside of the bedroom door, almost taking it off its hinges.

"Niamh, Niamh," he shouts, and this time there is danger in his voice. Inside, Niamh's eyes are consumed by fear.

"Open the door, Niamh, or it will be a lot worse for you in the end."

Niamh throws the receiver of the telephone aside and rushes towards the door to try to prevent him breaking through. Just as she nears the door Proctor hits it with his shoulder for a second time and succeeds in breaking in.

Niamh backs away again. Proctor stands menacingly in the doorway, his eyes filled with danger and malice. His list of options now has been narrowed down to one. He steps into the room and Niamh backs away from him: she is totally in the grip of fear. The backs of her knees now make contact with the end of the bed and she falls backwards on to the mattress. Proctor seizes the opportunity, leaps forward and lands heavily on top of her. His two hands are fixed firmly around her neck and he is squeezing hard, pressing both his thumbs against her windpipe. Niamh hasn't got the strength to fight him off. Her vision is blurring, then clearing, then blurring yet again: overhead, Proctors's face seems distorted – cloudy, indistinct; much uglier now than she had ever thought before. She is just about to succumb when she hears the siren of the patrol car. Or is it something she is imagining? Just then, Proctor eases his grip on her neck and Niamh hears the siren louder still. Then the sound of the front door being broken in and the tramp of feet rushing up the stairs . . .

HEREDITY

It had been the usual racket again all night long: Paul's father bickering, sniping, jibing from the moment he came in from the pub. It started out as always it seemed to – a dig about one thing or another to throw Paul's mother off her guard. One could deal with that, if that was the extent of it. But it was the absolute change in the father's personality that really got to them. As soon as he had a few drinks on him he became a totally different man. When on the dry he was pleasant, cheerful, funny even – life-and-soul-of-the-party type. But let a drop pass his lips and he became a changed person. Chalk and cheese. Surly. Quarrelsome. Bitter.

Paul had stayed up sitting and talking with his mother before his father arrived home. That too was pretty much as usual – each keeping the other company. Over the years, on nights like this, they had never actually got around to discussing his father's problem in any open sense; no overt mention of the trouble generated between Paul's father and mother because of the drink. Nonetheless, there was scarcely a time when Paul's mother didn't make some indirect reference to it.

"Whatever you do in later life, Paul, love, for God's sake stay clear of that bloody bottle," she'd say. "It does nothing but create trouble and heartbreak all round."

Trouble and heartbreak, for sure. The poor woman could write a book on either of them. She had endured seventeen long years of it at this stage – each year worse than the one that went before it.

"When you marry, Paul, always treat your wife as a wife deserves to be treated. Be gentle towards her, and understanding," she'd advise. "Ah sure, what am I saying at all," she'd say then, as though rebuking herself, "sure, God knows, you, of all people, wouldn't hurt a fly. You're not like . . . " and then she'd stop and say no more.

Later, when his father eventually arrived, Paul would head off to bed and leave his parents to their conversation. Conversation! – Huh! *Bombersation* was more like it.

Paul's bedroom was directly above the sitting-room and, try as he might, it was virtually impossible for him to miss a single syllable of the jibing that was going on below. For years it had been a game of psychological bullying and he, in his silence, had found it every bit as disturbing as had his mother. Despite turning up the volume on the clock-radio by his bedside, the taunting still got through. Jibing, jibing – and then the orders. "I'll have my dinner when I'm finished the last can." Yes, that was one of his father's more usual orders. Christ! Dinner at midnight, after his mother had gone to so much trouble to prepare it hours earlier, never knowing whether or not this could be a night that he might come home early. And God help her if, for any reason, the dinner was a little cold: all hell would break loose. And even worse again if it was dried up by the heat. A bully. Nothing but an out-and-out bully. A boor.

But last night's performance had been worse than any that Paul could remember. For some reason or other, it had really got to him more deeply than ever before. It may have been a combination of factors: the impending Leaving Cert. – now just three weeks away – was very much on his mind, and, at this stage, he found it hard to suppress his anger at the many study sessions that had been disrupted by his father's drinking. And then, always niggling at the back of his mind, there was the knowledge of how badly his mother was being treated.

It was some time in the middle of the night that he woke. He could hear them bickering in the bedroom next to his. The usual litany of abuse from his father and then the odd, short retort from his mother when she could hold her patience no longer. That went on for a while before he hit her. One solitary thump and she was silenced. And the father's thwarted need fully satiated.

And then the silence. A deafening silence. The only thing in flux now was Paul's own mind – racing, turning, replaying the turmoil over and over again; seething with anger towards this man who called himself a father. He was incensed at the hardship that had been inflicted on his mother; incensed at himself that it wasn't in his make-up to stand up to his father's violence.

"You're only a softie, a wimp – a bloody wimp, that's

all you are. Christ, you'll wise up in time, me bucko. You'll never get through life being a bloody softie."

He remembered the day his father had said that to him. It certainly wasn't that he had any regard for what his father did or didn't think of him and yet, as he lay there in the darkness, he could not but be aware that it was that very softness in his nature that prevented him from doing what he might like to do. Another sleepless night. He twisted this way and that in the bed, then turned on to his side and felt the wetness of the pillow press his tears back against his cheek.

When Paul wakes up next morning there isn't a stir in the house. He may feel he's had a sleepless night but, at some point in the brightening morning hours, exhaustion must have caught up with him, then eased him into sleep. The clock-radio reads 11.09 am. Christ, school! Half the morning is gone already. It wouldn't be worth his while going in at this point. And anyway, all he has after lunch is the one session of French. He won't bother – French is one of his stronger subjects.

Out of bed. Memories of last night are filing through his mind. The anger. The frustration. His mother. His gentle mother. Today is Friday: she'll be home early from work. He'll tidy up the place a bit before she gets in. God, isn't it bad enough that she has to go out to other people's houses to clean up their dirt for them without having to face back into it in her own place when she gets home. He'll have the place sparkling when she gets in. Then they can both sit and enjoy a cup of coffee together and natter a little for a while before he gets into doing a bit of study. Of course, last night's events won't even get a mention, he thinks, but that, unfortunately, is the way things are between them.

True to form, nothing is said. As they drink their coffee, his mother doesn't even mention the bruising around her eye. In fact, it is all the more obvious to Paul because she has tried to cover it up with powder. But he makes no reference to it either – that is as is best. And so, both just sit there civilly, sipping coffee and busily pretending that neither of them notices anything. But Paul finds it difficult to keep his peace. It is this very pretence over the years that has led to her being marked like this – beaten, bruised: his mother. It kills him to see her like this. Worse still is the fact that he doesn't have what it takes to rectify the situation. And he knows deep down just what it would take.

"Come on, love – off you go upstairs and get a few hours study in before dinner-time," she says. "Dad should be home by six, I'd say."

And, just for a second, when she refers to Dad, Paul is tempted to bring up the matter of the night before and force his mother to confront the issue of what is happening to her. But the moment's hesitation steals the opportunity away from him again.

"Yes, I'd better, I suppose," he says. "A few hours study can't do much harm at this stage . . . "

But very little in the line of study happens upstairs. Paul knows his own form by now. He puts in the time right enough, a book of one sort or another open there before him, but study isn't number one on his agenda. It's the same old story once again: this battering of his mother tormenting him, distracting him, playing itself over and over again in his mind. He'd gladly accept failure in the Leaving if only some solution to the problem could be found.

Time passes but, where study is concerned, nothing has changed except that one book has been substituted for another. Paul is seething within, allowing the venom that he feels towards his father to fester on itself. A quick glance at the clock: 6.53 pm. His mother is downstairs, still waiting for his father to arrive. Already the dinner has been put back an hour so that all three of them can dine together. To hell with him, thinks Paul. Some father! Some husband!

7.00 pm. Down the stairs comes Paul and into the kitchen. His mother is there, her back to him as she busies herself in an effort to keep her mind off other things. She turns around now and Paul can see the tears welling in her eyes. Years of tears. Tears of loneliness. Tears of fear. Paul comes to her and hugs her tightly, trying, if he can, to fill her heart with courage, to restore some little bit of that self-confidence that the troubled years have stolen from her.

"Come on, Mam, let's go ahead and eat. Dad can have his when he arrives."

A half-smile creeps across his mother's face and she nods her head in agreement with Paul's suggestion. And then the tears fall. Years of tears.

Though little is said as they eat, the silence itself speaks far more than words can do. The tears tell their own tale. A tear for every time she has been so cruelly abused over the past seventeen long years.

Paul lets his mother cry. It is a release that has been a

long time coming and, now that it has finally happened, it is as well to allow it run its course.

Paul clears off the table, takes the dishes out to the kitchen and, some minutes later, returns with a cup of coffee for his mother. She has moved away from the table and has fallen asleep in the only easy chair in the room – "Father's chair", as it is most often called. Her head is lying to one side, but, even in her sleep, the stress is very visible on her face. Paul leaves down the coffee, removes the light crocheted blanket from the back of one of the ordinary chairs and gently spreads it across his mother, tucking it in between the arm-rests and the cushion of the chair. He stands back then and looks at her; a gentle woman, a kindly woman. And then he feels the tears well up in his own eyes. "You're only a softie, a wimp – a bloody wimp," he again remembers his father saying.

A softie! If so, then it is his mother's softness he has inherited. His mother's gentleness. He looks at her again. He'll leave her sleeping for now and head back to the books again.

Upstairs, he looks at the book open on the desk before him: *A History of Europe: The Russian Campaign of Napoleon Bonaparte*. If he manages to absorb a single detail, that's about the height of it. His mind is every bit as addled as earlier – perhaps even more so. And full of venom. Venom mounting, seething in his mind again. Venom towards his father. All his thoughts now are born of anger and he is more incapable than ever of doing his study.

His mind focuses on his father's cruelty, his

bullishness. Nastiness, violences, abuse – each and every trait that smacks of negativity and churlishness he attributes to the father. Venom and anger feed off each other, and now Paul's own thinking is negative and filled with enmity towards his father. He feels disgust at the tyrannical mistreatment that his mother has been made to endure. The bastard.

It is the noise of the key in the hall-door lock below that distracts Paul from his negative musings. Immediately he looks over towards the clock: my God! 11.48 pm. Where has the night gone? Another night of so-called study down the drain.

Already, down below, his father has started to stir up trouble. More of the usual taunting. Paul can feel himself tense up. The jibing continues a little while, then his mother answers back for the first time. And then the jibing intensifies all the more. Then the second answer. Paul's own uneasiness intensifies. And the usual empty pontification from his father goes on down below. The image of his mother's bitter tears of earlier that afternoon comes to Paul's mind. The redness of her eyes – his mother's eyes. Father's eyes. Paul's own eyes. He goes over to the mirror to see the anger in his own eyes. His face is red and, as he looks into the mirror, he winces, distorting his appearance. But the eyes. There is something in his eyes that he cannot identify; something that he has never noticed there before.

The noise below is louder than ever and foremost in his mind now is the turmoil of the previous night. The memory of that thump into his mother's face in the secrecy of the night; the memory of the years of cruelty.

He looks into the mirror once again. Each trait that earlier he had seen in his own face seems even sharper now – more honed, more troubled. Again the jibing down below invades his mind. It is as though his head is in a vice – tightening, tightening, tightening. Then, suddenly, he explodes.

Paul bursts out from his room and bounds flat-footed down the stairway, taking several steps at a time. He'll put an end to this stupid carry-on; he'll finally face down all this cruelty and taunting. He rounds the banister at the bottom of the stairs and makes headlong for the sitting-room door. Something strange has taken him over. He pushes in the door with all his might and abruptly brings his father's rantings to a halt. And there he stands between the jambs – Paul, the boy, the softie of the house, staring, challenging, waiting.

"What the hell do you think you're at?" – his father.

"Get out of the room, Mam," says Paul.

"But Paul, love . . . "

"Out, Mam – *now*."

His mother looks over at her husband, but his eyes and Paul's are fixed firmly on one another.

"Now, Mam – out." This time she goes.

As soon as his mother passes by him, Paul pulls the sitting-room door shut and looks at his father once again. Their eyes lock. Paul allows the memories to fill his mind again, inviting them to feed the venom he has been feeling. Venom. Anger. Hatred. And now he realises that his father can see in his own son's eyes that element which Paul himself could not identify when, upstairs, he had seen it in the mirror. For the first time ever in his life the father sees something of his own nature in Paul's eyes. His immediate inclination is to get out of the room, but Paul is at the doorway. The father backs away a little and, as he does so, Paul surges forward violently . . .